MW00814935

13 DEADLY ENDINGS

THOMAS M. MALAFARINA

Mechanicsburg, PA USA

Published by Sunbury Press, Inc.
Mechanicsburg, Pennsylvania

www.sunburypress.com

For information about special discounts for bulk purchases, please contact Sunbury Press Orders Dept. at (855) 338-8359 or orders@sunburypress.com.

To request one of our authors for speaking engagements or book signings, please contact Sunbury Press Publicity Dept. at publicity@sunburypress.com.

ISBN: 978-1-62006-794-9 (Trade paperback)
ISBN: 978-1-62006-795-6 (Mobipocket)

Library of Congress Control Number: 2016961936

FIRST SUNBURY PRESS EDITION: December 2016

Product of the United States of America
0 1 1 2 3 5 8 13 21 34 55

Set in Bookman Old Style
Designed by Crystal Devine
Cover by Amber Rendon
Edited by Allyson Gard

Continue the Enlightenment!

DEDICATION

For the love of my life, my amazing wife JoAnne.
All of my love and thanks is not nearly enough to
express my appreciation for all you do to allow my
strange literary adventure to continue and flourish.

INTRODUCTION

In July of 2010 Sunbury Press released my second book, a short story collection called, *13 Nasty Endings*. It was part of a three-book deal consisting of *99 Souls, 13 Nasty Endings* and *Burn Phone*. *99 Souls* and *Burn Phone* were both novels. As it turned out, these three books were just the tip of a very large iceberg. Since that time I have written numerous novels and over one hundred short stories as of October 2016.

One of the problems facing these early works besides the fact that I was new to writing novels and publishing was editing. Most complaints of these works have been that the stories themselves were great but the editing left a lot to be desired. In Sunbury's defense, I should explain that at the time these works were released, Sunbury was a very small company trying to grow. As such they didn't have the excellent editors they now have available.

In my own defense . . . well, I suppose I have no defense. I'll be the first to tell you that I have tons of excellent ideas for horror stories and I'm more than a half-decent writer. However, I've always been a terrible speller and my punctuation stinks as well. I've gotten better over the years but I still leave a lot to be desired. If it weren't for spelling and grammar checkers, my literary output would be a fraction of what it currently is. I'd be spending all my time looking up the spelling of every other word and rewriting manuscripts.

I often joke that having been born and raised in the town of Ashland in Schuylkill County Pennsylvania, English is actually my second language; coal-speak is my first. Excuses aside, for years I've wanted to rework at least those first three books; *99 Souls, 13 Nasty Endings* and *Burn Phone.* In early December of 2015 I met with my publisher over dinner to discuss my books and we agreed I would re-write and re-edit the first three books. Then Sunbury Press would, officially re-edit the books and reissue all three of them with new titles and new covers to help create and solidify a recognizable brand. We felt this might also help to direct attention to some of my earlier works for people who were unfamiliar with my writing. We also decided to use whatever cover scheme we developed across the entire family of my books. So I started the project of reworking them. I looked at them with fresh eyes that hadn't read them in years. I wanted to see if the stories still held up at their 5-year anniversary. I was surprised how little work I had to do. As I anticipated there was lots of editing and some reworking involved, but all in all I felt they held up nicely.

What you'll be reading on the following pages is *13 Deadly Endings.* This is the reworked version of what had originally been called *13 Nasty Endings.* If you have never read it before, I hope it meets your expectations. If you read the original, I hope you like the new and improved all the better. Enjoy.

Thomas M. Malafarina
October 2016

FOR ETERNITY

Sandra sat looking at herself in the hotel vanity mirror absolutely beaming with delight. She wasn't the type of woman who was prone to lie to herself, accepting she was no raving beauty. Similarly, she wasn't what one might consider a hideous troll. Nevertheless, she understood she had a slightly below average looking face and had about a hundred or more extra pounds she could stand to lose. On the positive side, she did possess a good personality, was very easy to get along with and was willing to please.

Yet still she couldn't comprehend how she ever could have been so lucky as to land such a tall, handsome, good looking and successful man as Brad Stratford. To think they had only met three months earlier and now she was in the honeymoon suite of one the most luxurious hotels in Las Vegas and was now Mrs. Bradley Fenton Stratford III.

The whirlwind courtship had rapidly blossomed into a torrid love affair and had concluded with the couple's eloping against her parent's wishes. Sandra didn't really care what her parents thought. She was, after all, almost thirty years old and could do as she pleased when she pleased. Her parents would have to understand, and she was sure someday they'd grow to love Brad as much as she did. Her father said Brad was a gold-digger after her money even though she tried to explain Brad was very successful and had plenty of his own money.

She looked out into the main living room of the suite seeing Brad on his cell phone. "The poor man" she thought. "He works so hard in order to be successful. If he only knew how much money, I'll soon inherit. Perhaps someday when he does he'll learn to slow down a little bit."

Marvin Wallace Slotnick, a.k.a. Bradley Fenton Stratford III paced about the honeymoon suit going through the motions of appearing to be talking with an important client on his cell phone when in fact he wasn't speaking with anyone. Marvin/Brad was a con man and not only was he anything but successful, but was actually flat broke.

He looked back toward the dressing area of the suite and saw Sandra looking at him like a little lost puppy. He smiled pantomimed blowing a kiss and thought, "How did I ever end up married to such a disgusting sow as that?"

Up until recently, he had been a minor league hustler satisfied to make a few thousand bucks and therefore never hurting for cash until recently, and now he had accidentally stumbled into the major leagues.

Marvin had never taken a con this far before. Usually he'd meet a homely trust-fund chick with low self-esteem and sell her his story about being a successful financial advisor. He'd wine and dine her get her to fall in love with him and get his hands on her money. Then he'd take off in the dead of night never to be seen again.

With Sandra, things had not been quite as easy and had quickly gotten out of control. Although he knew she was allotted over a quarter of a million a year from a trust fund, plenty for him to con from her, he learned by snooping through some of the documents in her penthouse apartment she also stood to inherit over twenty million when she turned thirty years old. That was less than a year away, and she had absolutely no idea he knew anything about it.

Sandra seemed to have fallen much harder and faster for him than any of the other girls had ever done, and she was an extremely jealous and possessive woman, a real suffocating clinging vine. She was also very high emotional maintenance. She was constantly telling him how much she loved him and he was the greatest thing to ever happen to her. She would also say how their love was so special and so strong it would last beyond their time on earth; it would last for eternity, blah, blah freaking blah.

Marvin took advantage of her enthusiasm of course and, being the sociopath he was, he used it to get an emotional hold on her even her parents couldn't break. He would tell her all the things she wanted to hear leading her to believe he had fallen head over heels in love with her as well.

So here, he was in the honeymoon suite married under a fake name, probably not even a legal marriage to a lovesick walking side of beef that was going to make the next year of his life a living Hell just by being part of it. She had even coerced him into going along with the idea of writing their own wedding vows, which she insisted should contain the phrase "for eternity" because she knew their love such as theirs was so strong not even death could separate them. He kept telling himself it would all be worth it someday soon when the big payoff came: twenty million smack-a-roonies.

But what to do about the parents. He had been certain the old man saw right through him and had been doing everything possible to convince Sandra to end the relationship. Marvin didn't know how much control the old man had over the inheritance either, which made things even trickier. He knew the actual money came from a grandfather who apparently once owned several companies, had been a gazillionaire and had set up trust fund and inheritance for all his children and grandchildren, Sandra being one of the latter.

Marvin knew it was going to be a long and painful year, but he was determined to get in the old man's good graces in time for his beloved sea hag to get her inheritance. By then he'd have devised a plan to get his paws on the money and get out of Dodge.

He heard Sandra's cell phone ringing from inside the dressing area and saw her pick it up. She yelled out into the suite, "Brad, Honey that will be Mummy and Daddy. I left them a message earlier saying we ran off to get married." she twittered, "I can't wait to hear what they have to say." She said this knowing all Hell was about to break loose. Then she answered the phone, with a cheerful, "Hello."

Marvin was furious but tried to control himself by pacing around in the other room still pretending to be on an important call. That stupid bovine was going to screw up everything. He had to formulate a plan to try to smooth things over with the parents but knew the task would be daunting. Now thanks to his walrus wife the whole scheme could blow right out of the water.

He listened to her conversation while appearing to be busy with his own call. Things seemed to start smoothly enough but eventually Sandra started getting louder and Marvin could tell the old man had gotten on the line.

"Daddy? What are you saying? You're lying! How could you say such a thing? Proof? What proof?" She was now crying into the phone.

Marvin thought, "Oh boy, this can't be good." He continued to eavesdrop as her unhappiness turned to anger.

"You did what? A private investigator? Why would you do that? He's lying, Daddy. He's just telling you what he knows you want to hear. Fine! Go right ahead! Then do it if it makes you feel good! What do I care? We don't need the money. Bradley has plenty of his own."

"Oh no!" Marvin thought to himself, "She's really going to screw this up big time."

She continued, "I don't care, Daddy. What? Then we'll live on love, Daddy. Good bye!" She disconnected the cell phone and walked tearfully out to Marvin setting the phone on a nearby end table. Marvin took her in his arms pretending to console her all the while trying to figure out how to repair the damage she had just done.

"Daddy was absolutely horrible, Brad." She cried, "He tried to tell me all sorts of lies about you saying your name wasn't Bradley Fenton Stratford III and you were some sort of con-man named Marvin Slotnick. How could he be so cruel as to make up such a lie? Then he threatened to not allow me to get my inheritance."

"Inheritance?" Marvin feigned ignorance. "What inheritance? You never said anything about any inheritance."

She continued, "I know I shouldn't have kept it from you, darling, but my grandfather left me a lot of money which I was supposed to inherit when I turn thirty. My trust fund comes from the interest on that money. Now, not only is Daddy going to get his lawyer to keep me from my inheritance, but he is going to cut off my trust fund monthly allotments as well. That is unless I agree to annul our marriage!" She started crying again.

Marvin tried to find a way to salvage this mess. If she didn't get that money, he was in major trouble. He said, "Sandra, my sweetness. You know I love you more than life itself. But it's wrong for me to be the cause of you missing out on what is rightfully yours. And it's wrong for you and your parents to quarrel. They truly love you and I'm sure they only want what's best for you. I'm the outsider here. I can't allow myself to come between you and them no matter how much we love each other. Maybe we rushed into this whole marriage thing. Maybe we should get it temporarily annulled and continue to see each other until your father comes around and learns to like me."

"That will never happen, Brad. Daddy has made up his mind about you and about the money. He's thickheaded about stuff like this. As long as we're married, I'll never get another penny. But I don't care. We don't need his money. We have your income and more importantly, we have each other. I told him we can live on love and our love will last for eternity."

Marvin's fury rose to an uncontrollable level at the realization he was stuck with this loathsome woman and they were now penniless. He pushed her away shouting, "You stupid lovesick fool! How could you be so idiotic as to throw away twenty million dollars?" Then too late, he realized his mistake.

"Brad? What did you just say to me? I never told you how much money I was getting." She asked hurtfully, "How . . . how did you know about it?"

Marvin stuttered, "I . . . I . . . I . . . I didn't know! I . . . I didn't know anything of the sort. I just pulled that number out of thin air." Then regaining some of his composure said, "I could have just as easily said ten or thirty million."

"But you didn't!" She insisted with realization and sorrow in her tear-filled eyes, "You said twenty million! You knew! Oh my God! Daddy was right! You are after my money!"

Marvin unsuccessfully made one last attempt to redirect the downward spiraling situation, "But, Sandra. Darling. You know I love you. That's all that matters."

"Don't say such things to me, Brad, or Marvin or whatever your real name is. We swore before God to love each other for eternity, and Heaven help me somehow still love you and I know part of me always will. But it's over, Brad. We can't be together. I'm calling Daddy. Now get out of here!"

Sandra turned, picked up her cell phone and got ready to call her parents. Marvin panicked grabbed a heavy iron lamp from the nearby table bringing it down hard on Sandra's skull. With a sickening cracking sound, she fell to the floor. Marvin bent down examining for signs of blood and found none. But he did notice a huge lump forming on the side of her head. He checked for a pulse and saw she was still alive but unconscious. This gave him an idea for a devious way to get out of this and perhaps still get at least some of what he wanted.

In the bathroom of the suite was an enormous tub made of solid marble. Marvin reached under Sandra's arms and dragged her unconscious body with great difficulty into the bathroom. He filled the tub with hot water adding scented bubble bath. Then he laboriously undressed his new bride, hoisted her naked body over the side of the tub allowing it to slide down under the water.

He stood over top of the tub, looking down in to the water watching the bubbles escaping from Sandra's nose and mouth. Soon he knew it would soon all be over and he could put the rest of his quickly devised plan in to motion.

Then unexpectedly Sandra's eyes opened wide and as she stared up at Marvin through the water in utter terror attempting to struggle to the surface. Marvin did the only thing he could think of and held Sandra's head down below the water as she frantically kicked and thrashed. After a few agonizing minutes the struggling stopped, and Marvin again looked down to see Sandra's lifeless eyes staring up through the water at him. He knew now she was most definitely dead, but the angry look still present in her dead eyes seemed to bore a hole right into his very soul. Marvin cleaned up around the area with towels and then finished formulating his plan.

Three months later, Marvin sat on a moving box in Sandra's apartment thinking about how easily he had gotten away with her murder and how he had managed to pull off the most rewarding con of his life. Although he never did get any of the twenty million, he had managed to do quite well for himself.

Unknown to Marvin, good old lovesick Sandra had made out a new will leaving Brad/Marvin the penthouse apartment, which was paid for and worth close to a million dollars. She also willed him the bulk of her estate which since she had not been a big spender ended up being another one and a half million. Later he found out she had named him as a beneficiary in her three million dollar life insurance policy. As if that wasn't enough, before they left for Vegas she had taken out a term policy for another three million dollars. Finally he had settled a lawsuit out of court with the hotel for an additional million. Life was good.

To say the least, Marvin now had more money than he had ever hoped to have in his life, and no one except for Sandra's father had suspected a thing. Marvin recounted the events following the murder. He did this often to make sure he hadn't missed anything. He knew Sandra's father was spending a small fortune on private investigators doing all he could to find evidence Marvin had murdered his little girl.

As soon as Marvin had cleaned up the spilled water around the tub, he had dressed and left the room making sure he wedged the door open with Sandra's key card. He immediately headed downstairs to the hotel restaurant making a point of speaking to as many hotel guests and staff members as possible happily telling them he was on his honeymoon and his lovely bride had chosen to order breakfast in and was probably soaking in a luxurious bath. He turned on all the charm he could muster making sure he made a memorable impression with everyone.

Once Marvin was certain he had established a good enough alibi, he went back to their room removed the wedge from the door then entered and using the room phone, disguised his voice to sound as much like a woman as possible while ordering a light plate of fruit from room service.

He immediately left the room, allowing the door to close and lock this time and hid in the stairwell at the end of the hall. When the elevator eventually opened and the room service attendant wheeled a cart toward his room door Marvin left the stairway and quietly walked behind the man. As the attendant knocked on the door Marvin spoke up pleasantly saying his wife mustn't have heard the knock and telling the man he had just returned from having breakfast downstairs. Taking his key card, he opened the door allowing the man and cart to enter. Marvin made sure to not thank or tip the attendant immediately so the man would stick around for a little while. He needed him as a witness.

Marvin made a show of walking around the suite calling Sandra's name in a loving manner then as he entered the adjacent bathroom he let out a terrifying scream crying, "Oh my God no!" as he pretended to discover his beloved bride had drown. He ran back to the room in tears pleading, "Help me! Something has happened to my wife!"

The rest was history. After a cursory investigation which included speaking to many of the witnesses who all vouched for Marvin's alibi, it was determined Sandra must have slipped and fallen while getting into the bath, struck her head and drowned.

Sandra's father had, of course raised a fuss and was still working to nail Marvin. Marvin had little doubt eventually the old man would find a way to get him legally or otherwise, but by then it would be too late. Marvin had already collected the insurance money and cleaned out Sandra's bank account putting it all into an offshore bank in a sunny tropical country having no extradition treaties with the United States. He had sold the apartment, and in less than a week, he would be on his way out of the country with a new name a new life and a ton of money.

"Thank you, Sandra, my beloved," he said aloud, "So much for you and your ridiculous fantasy about us being together for eternity." He chuckled to himself as he enjoyed a last drink in the penthouse. Tomorrow he was moving into a hotel until the real-estate settlement nonsense was over then he would be on his way.

As Marvin sat looking across the almost empty apartment, he thought he heard the dripping of water sounding surprisingly loud and foreboding, echoing through the hollow rooms. It sounded like it was coming from the kitchen. He got up and walked over to the sink seeing the faucet slowly dripping into the bowl. Drip, drip, drip. The thumping tone was practically maddening in the huge empty space.

Marvin looked down into the sink and couldn't believe his eyes. As each drip of water thudded against the stainless steel basin, they each formed an elliptical ball-shaped bead. Immediately each bead grew six transparent spider-like legs and quickly skittered away to make room for the next water droplet to fall repeating the process. Marvin saw each of the spider droplets had also grown round transparent heads with large mouths, each filled with hundreds of tiny needle like teeth. It was impossible! There had to be twenty or thirty of the skittering creatures in the sink and more arriving every second or two. Some of them merged forming what appeared to be transparent centipedes with mouths full of the teeth running along their backs.

Not thinking, Marvin reached into the sink pressing his left index finger against the back of one of the droplets expecting it to disintegrate under his touch. Instead, it immediately wrapped itself around the tip of his finger biting down, removing the skin and feasting on the blood flowing freely from the wound. The thing swelled up like a tick turning red with the newfound food source. It dropped to the bottom of the sink where several others of the creatures jumped on top of it forming a larger version of the first creature. The thing ran around the bottom of the sink picking up more droplets, growing in size and changing its shape.

Backing away from the sink in shock, Marvin grabbed some paper towels wrapping them around the wounded finger. He tugged on the handle of the faucet to stop the dripping but it wouldn't stop. The incessant noise from the steady dripping seemed to grow increasingly louder in his mind like Chinese water torture.

Behind him, he heard more dripping sounds coming from the bathroom. He raced into the room finding both the sink and tub dripping strangely in perfect time with the kitchen sink each drip producing more of the spider things. Looking down in to the tub Marvin saw some of these creatures had already merged together becoming larger than the ones in the kitchen, some of them resembling see-through rats with bloated bodies and longish snouts equipped with hundreds of long sharp teeth as well as huge paws with sharp transparent claws.

Stunned by the vision, Marvin didn't see one of the things jump up from the tub latching onto his nose before splashing to the floor. Pain surged through his injured face as he looked down to see some of the flesh from his nose at the bottom of the tub melting and absorbed by the horrid creatures. Blood poured down his face into his mouth. He spat the flowing blood down into the tub where the many smaller spider things still dripping from the faucet quickly lapped it up.

Marvin knew what was happening wasn't even remotely possible yet it was happening. He saw the rat-thing sitting in the corner feasting on another scrap from his nose. His fury grew red-hot, and he attempted to swat the awful creature with his open right palm.

The thing flattened out under the impact of Marvin's hand then immediately wrapped itself up around the hand dissolving the flesh and absorbing it faster than if he had put his hand in a vat of acid. Within seconds, he was looking at a skeleton where his hand once had been; pieces of flesh and muscle dripping to the floor where more of the tiny creatures were quickly absorbing the feast. Then the remaining bones began to disintegrate turning to dust and falling away. He bellowed from the incredible pain and unbelievable horror. Blood now flowed freely from the stump.

Looking toward the tub and sink Marvin saw thousands of the smaller water creatures were climbing up over the rim down the sides and making it to the floor. Some of them had grouped together forming something resembling a transparent human hand using its fingers to pull itself across the floor toward him.

Before he could react, the hand thing raced across the room plunging straight into the crotch of his pants immediately turning his genitalia into a gelatinous blood and flesh soup. He looked down in horror seeing a gaping hole where his crotch had been. He screamed in agony rolling over and attempting to crawl back to the main living room away from the horrible things all the while trailing streaks of blood behind him.

He crawled weakly into the center of the apartment back toward the shipping crate he found himself surrounded by the water creatures some still transparent but many bloated and red with his precious life blood.

Marvin saw creatures approaching him from both, the bathroom and the kitchen, their numbers growing as he continued to bleed providing them with yet more nourishment. He didn't know what to do next as he lie on the floor injured, weak, bleeding and unable to defend himself from the next attack which he knew would be coming soon.

Suddenly all of the water creatures in their various shapes and sizes began to lose their structure and merge together, forming a huge body of liquid encircling Marvin. Thin tendrils of water reach out like hideous straws sucking up every drop of blood from the floor around Marvin, but for whatever reason they seemed to leave him alone. He suspected they were going to wait for him to bleed to death. He looked toward the bathroom and the kitchen seeing the tiny spider creatures were continuing to form and work their way into the living room merging with the main flow increasing its size. The giant water circle was translucent pink with flowing ribbons of darker red all courtesy of Marvin's own blood.

Then Marvin thought he heard someone call his name, or more precisely Brad's name. He was taken aback for a moment, and then he thought perhaps he had been delirious from blood loss and was imagining the sound, when he heard it again.

"Bradley." The voice called and may God forgive him he recognized the voice. It was Sandra's.

Looking out toward the water mass in front of him Marvin saw a pair of dark blood-red lips rising up from the surface of the water. The lips moved attempting to call him again then sank back down into the water. Then he saw fingertips and then a watery hand rising up out of the horrible fluid and after a second or two losing its structure and liquefying back into the mass.

Staring in amazement Marvin saw something new rising up from the liquid; not just rising but actually pulling the watery mass along up with it not leaving a single water droplet behind.

The thing was incredible, towering close to eight feet in size and about ten feet across it cylindrical "body," an enormous vortex of rapidly swirling bloody liquid. Near the top of the tornado-like mass, Marvin first saw the lips reappear then a nose then an entire face came forth from the spinning maelstrom. It was Sandra's face as smooth as glass amid the chaotic liquid turmoil. The face opened its eyes and once again, Marvin saw the same accusatory look he had seen staring at him from the bottom of the bathtub the day he had killed her. The lips began to move and he heard the fluid voice of the Sandra thing speaking to him; its sounds like those of someone trying to speak while gargling. "Hello, Bradley. I came back for you," the creature said.

"What do you want from me, Sandra?" Marvin cried. "I didn't mean to kill you, I swear. I lost my temper and panicked. I am so sorry." Marvin had managed to sit up his back resting against a shipping box.

The Sandra creature looked angrily down at the dying man declaring, "You swore before God we would be together for eternity. Now we will be." As the thing continued to stare down at him, its face fading in and out of its liquid form a huge tendril emerged from a the base of the swirling water spout.

The snake-like appendage danced in the air in front of Marvin. At the end of the tentacle, he saw a pair of lips begin to form. He looked up and saw the Sandra face was now gone the huge waterspout had moved downward. The lips parted revealing an enormous mouth filled with rows of razor sharp teeth like those of a shark.

With immeasurable speed, the snake thing flew straight for Marvin's crotch entering him through the gaping wound where his genitalia had once been and using his own bloodstream as a superhighway, spread itself quickly throughout his body.

Marvin began to convulse and shake uncontrollably as trickling streams of blood began to flow from every orifice and pore in his body. Rivulets of blood streamed from his eye sockets as his eyeballs turned to jelly, sloughing down his cheeks burning furrows in his face, which was also losing its shape. His blackened tongue fell from his mouth and before it hit the floor it was quickly snatched from the air by a thin tentacle of water and pulled into the body of the snake thing.

Bloody water trickled from Marvin's ears immediately turning back into hundreds of spider creatures began feasting on is dissolving face. His clothing sagged in upon itself as his body turned to soup and his bones disintegrated.

Marvin's conscious mind should have died long before his body did, but Sandra had chosen to keep him aware as long as possible. She had to teach naughty Bradley a lesson. He needed to understand, although she still loved him with all of her heart and soul, she was in charge of this new relationship and wouldn't permit any misbehavior on his part. After all, they were now going to be together, for eternity.

BUZZARDS

Harry was one of those individuals who never seemed to pay attention to anything for very long. His wife constantly bugged him about what she thought of as his negative trait, but he never seemed to mind her criticism. He understood there was nothing he could do to change the way he was; it was just his way. He had a very short attention span and almost no ability to focus for very long.

As far back as Harry could remember, he had always been that way. In grade school, his teachers knew he was a "bright boy," but they often became frustrated with his lack of focus. So at parent-teacher nights they would take the opportunity to all tell his mother basically the same story. They would each say, "Harry could be an A-student if he would just learn to focus and apply himself instead of allowing himself to be so distracted with nonsense all the time."

Harry was just a few months away from turning fifty-five; double nickels or speed limit as his friends liked to refer to that particular chronological milestone. And despite the span of years since he had been a young boy, he was still battling his ability to concentrate. In fact, while he was supposed to be focusing on his driving on that particular evening, he was busy thinking about three or four work related subjects while simultaneously listening to a CD and fiddling with his new cell phone. But then again that was Harry.

It was late Friday evening close to midnight, and Harry was heading home following a very long and stressful day of working. After leaving his day job, he had stopped by to put in a few hours at his part-time job. As a result, he was extremely tired. He was having more than his normal share of problems, focusing and to make matters worse, no sooner had he left work than it started pouring down rain.

He was driving along a two-lane road over a mountaintop through a wooded area, which eventually sloped downhill before finally reaching his subdivision. A full moon illuminated the road with an eerie glow despite the rain and the cloud cover.

Just before the crest of the mountain, there was a sharp left curve. Busy focusing on his other activities, Harry entered the curve at a speed too fast for conditions. As he rounded the turn, he saw something up ahead causing him to stomp his brake pedal down to the floor sending his car into a hydroplaning forward slide. The events, which occurred in the next five or six seconds happened in what seemed like slow motion as a thousand thoughts flashed across Harry's consciousness making the event feel more like several minutes.

Standing on the brake pedal, his hands in a death grip on the steering wheel, Harry looked through the rain-soaked windshield and saw something in the middle of the road up ahead. Within a fraction of a second, his mind took in everything. At first, he thought perhaps he was imagining things. He saw what looked like a man perhaps six feet tall with a bald fleshy head, wearing some sort of dark cloak kneeling down in the middle of the road. The man's face appeared to be buried deep in some type of road kill, like he was feasting on the vile flyblown carcass like it was a gourmet meal.

Oddly, Harry found himself wondering about what type of road kill it might be; like such a thought actually had any bearing on the current situation. Was it a ground hog? A skunk? A fox? A cat? A dog? Then coming back into focus he began to wonder what that man was thinking, eating some maggot infested road pizza, which had probably been baking in the hot July sun all day long?

"Get out of the way!" Harry screamed aloud at the vagrant as his mind rapidly conjured up images of him on trial for vehicular homicide, his entire life ruined because of some homeless maggot-eating bum.

Harry tried desperately to control the skidding vehicle and saw the man turning, seeing the oncoming car, his eyes glowing radiantly in the headlights. It was at that moment Harry realized what he was seeing wasn't a man at all but some sort of colossal bird. As the car got closer to the thing, Harry saw what he mistook for a dark cloak was actually a huge pair of folded wings. The creature spread its enormous wings, and Harry was shocked to see the wingspan was well over twenty feet from end to end.

In the final second or two as Harry's car skidded toward the creature, it took flight but unfortunately was just a millisecond too late. As Harry's car passed over the road kill, the huge bird had climbed to a height just above the hood and a fraction of a moment later the thing crashed headlong into the windshield.

Harry closed his eyes just before the impact and heard the shattering of glass as the huge thing collided into and then traveled right through the windshield. Harry's car came to a stop a few feet later, and Harry sat with his eyes closed for a brief time not sure, if he was alive or dead and strangely still wondering about what type of animal the road kill had been.

"Focus, Harry, focus," he thought to himself. That statement had become something of a mantra for him throughout his life and had helped him to regain his concentration many times in the past.

Harry slowly opened his eyes unsure if wanted to see what kind of damage the monstrous bird had done to his car. He knew by the sounds, and by how his body ached from the tug of the seatbelt, the accident was a bad one. His car had stalled, and he was sitting in darkness with only the limited light from the clouded moon to help him see. The windshield directly in front of him was shattered into a spider web of tiny cracks, while blackness shrouded the rest of the windshield from the giant beast he assumed lay dead on the hood of the car.

He reached his right hand down and released his seat belt, which sprang past him returning to its cradle startling him. He grabbed the door handle trying to get the door open, but it seemed to have been jammed shut by the impact of the collision.

"Just how big was this beast?" he wondered. Though the door wouldn't open it did release just far enough for the interior light to come on. Harry had to catch his breath and keep himself from screaming after seeing what the light unveiled.

The incredible creature had not only struck the windshield, but its massive head had come right through the shattered glass and was dangling at the end of its long thick neck into the interior of the car. Harry was astonished at the amazing size of the thing. Its pink flesh-covered neck was almost two feet long from where the feathered body lay outside the windshield to the place where an almost human-size head hung down below the dashboard on the passenger side of the car. The top of the thing's skull had a long gaping lesion, a severed flap of bloody flesh hanging loosely, blood streaming from the wound.

The neck appeared to be impossibly as thick as a full-grown man's. Harry looked to where the thing's neck met its body at the shattered windshield and saw a huge gash from which pools of blood flowed freely. Obviously, an artery was severed. As if in slow motion, the blood ran along the length of the neck then steadily dripped down onto the passenger side floor. Harry felt nauseous for a moment then managed to regain his composure.

Harry had never seen such a colossal beast in his life and stared at the thing in awe, trying to determine just what kind of creature it was. It appeared to be some sort of buzzard or vulture with a dark brown and black feathered body and a wrinkled pink colored neck and fleshy head. He couldn't see its facial features as its head hung down below his field of vision. Having seen smaller versions of birds such as this he knew it must have a large hooked beak, which would be very sharp for ripping the flesh from the carrion, which would be its source of food. He was thankful the beast was dead or else he might have found himself in more trouble than he could possibly handle trapped in the limiting space of the car.

The smell from the creature was beyond revolting, stinking of both animal and decomposing flesh thanks to the horrid thing's diet. Harry turned the ignition key one click to see if he could get the side window to go down, which fortunately it did. He pushed the steering wheel adjustment button and lifted the wheel out of his way then grabbed the upper frame of the window twisting his body sideways preparing to lift himself out of the opening. As he sat crossways in the seat his arms up holding the top of the car and his legs still under the driver's console he looked again at the massive creature in wonder and then thought for a moment he saw it move.

He froze in place watching the beast for any other sign of life. Then he heard a slight snuffling sort of noise coming from the thing. "Oh, my sweet Lord Jesus!" Harry thought, muffling horrified cry. "It's waking up."

Harry pulled his legs as far away from the thing as he could, being careful not to make too much noise. The last thing Harry wanted was to be helpless in the claustrophobic confines of his car while some mutated crazy creature ripped him to bits.

The thing slowly turned its head in Harry's direction, its left eye glowing with a red-hot fury born of Hell itself. Its right eye was gone with a huge shard of glass protruding from the bloody-black opening. Blood continued to pour from its neck and started to spurt as the creature became awake. It weakly lifted its head allowing Harry to see a full view of its horrific face. It appeared to be some sort of buzzard or vulture, but then again it seemed to have some human qualities as well; an intelligent awareness the likes of which he hadn't expected from a wild beast.

The creature continued raising its head until it was above the dashboard its human/buzzard skull with its razor sharp hooked beak staring angrily at Harry with its one good blood red eye. Its face was a mass of cuts with broken bits of glass protruding from the wounds.

Then without warning, it attacked. The buzzard creature lashed out at Harry with a fury and speed he never could have anticipated from such a badly wounded creature. He attempted to plaster himself against the driver's door but was a fraction of a second too late. Though barely able to reach him, the beak of the beast managed to rip a hole across Harry's shirt, tearing a half-inch wide gouge in his flesh across the width of his substantial stomach. Blood poured from the gash, and his flesh burned with an incredible fire.

The creature again lifted its mangled head ready for another attack, but then its eye began to glaze over as its head slowly slumped down. The creature was too weak from blood loss to attempt another strike. Harry took advantage of the opportunity and started to pull himself from the car. Then incredibly, he heard a raspy high-pitched voice calling to him. "You!" the voice shouted before trailing off into a sickening wheeze.

Harry again looked at the battered human-like face of the dying buzzard. "What?" He questioned, "What did you say?" He couldn't believe he was even asking such a question of the dying wild creature.

Again the thing glared weakly at Harry and incredibly responded with the same whining cry, "You, You keelt meee. Now I keelt you." The voice faded as the creature uttered it final gasp, dying; its head falling down and dangling above the floor of the car.

"What the Hell?" Harry shouted while simultaneously pulling himself up and out of the window, his shredded abdomen in agony from the creature's vicious attack. He fell out the window landing hard on the ground smashing his right arm and possibly breaking it. Then using the car door for support he stumbled weakly to his feet. He stood for a moment on wobbly legs, his arm aching, feeling weak, almost like he was under the influence of some strange drug. It was as if the buzzard thing had not just wounded him but had also contaminated him with some type of venom.

The last words of the creature echoed in his mind, "You, You keelt meee. Now I keelt you."

Harry looked around him hoping another car might pass by to render aid, but there was no sign of anyone on the empty desolate road. He noticed at least the rain had stopped and the cloud cover was breaking allowing the moon to shine brightly.

He looked across the hood of his car stunned by the incredible size of the dead creature. No wonder his car was wrecked; hitting the thing was like slamming into a brick wall. Thank goodness he had worn his seat belt or he might have been killed instantly.

Then, once again, in his mind he heard the buzzard's cry "You, you keelt meee. Now I keelt you." It was unfortunate his car wasn't equipped with air bags or maybe the thing wouldn't have been able to get close enough to gouge him the way it had.

Harry began walking down the sloping road toward his home unbuttoning his shirt to examine his scalding wound in the moonlight. Blood continued to pour freely from the gash, and Harry could feel himself getting weaker by the minute. He stripped off his shirt, wadding it up to use as a compress trying to stem the flow of his precious life blood. He pulled out his cell phone to try to call for help but saw there was no service this high up on the mountain. He checked his stomach again.

As he studied his wound in the moonlight his view was momentarily blocked by a shadow crossing overhead. Harry looked up but saw nothing. He staggered forward a few steps and noticed the shadow blocking the light again; first it was there then it was gone and then it was back again.

Harry looked up toward the glowing moon which was still partially hidden behind a few lingering clouds. Then he saw them; five, no ten, maybe more, enormous buzzards like the one he had just killed soaring high above the trees, circling, encircling him.

He knew he had to make an attempt to get home which was only two or three miles away, but he was so very weak; his vision blurring as he plodded aimlessly down the sloping road, staggering from side to side. Blood ran down this stomach saturating his pants. Harry felt the warmth of his blood running down his legs. Finally, those same legs gave out and he fell to the hard asphalt face first, breaking his nose and knocking out several of his teeth. More of his precious blood pooled on the ground next to his battered face. Delirious, he rolled over onto his back, the blood now gurgling in his throat.

He could see them circling, swooping ever closer. He knew then they were coming, coming for him. He had taken one of theirs, and now they would simply wait for him to die and pick him to pieces. His last thoughts were of the final words of the huge buzzard creature: "You, you keelt meee. Now I keelt you." and the last thing he saw was the moon completely blotted out by the many wings of the enormous buzzards.

BRIGHT OF THE LIVING DEAD

The world as it once was no longer existed. Planet Earth was crawling with maggot infested flesh-eating creatures the press gave the suitable name "zombies" in honor of the monsters depicted in George Romero's movie, *Night Of The Living Dead*.

The similarity to the horrifying creatures from that early horror movie was remarkable, as if somehow Mr. Romero had the ability to see into the future. Also, unlike the quick-moving undead creatures in the countless zombie spin-off movies which were produced in the forty years following Romero's ground breaking film, (no pun intended), these actual zombies lumbered around mindlessly at a slow pace similar to how they were pictured in his original film.

It was hard to comprehend it had only been a few short months since the first dead body had clawed its way out of its grave then plodded across the cemetery grounds then ripped out the throat of the elderly groundskeeper. The creature left the devastated remains of the old man nothing more than a human jigsaw puzzle of dismembered limbs, innards and chunks of torn flesh, his brain sucked completely out of his aged skull. The media promptly called that particular event "Zombie Ground Zero."

It wasn't long until countless other formerly dead souls around the globe began to climb from their graves or simply got up from their deathbeds to roam the lands in search of living human flesh to devour. One thing they all seemed to have in common was an insatiable need to consume the living.

At first, the authorities believed they had the so-called "plague" under control. A plague was how they preferred to classify the phenomena although no viruses or germs had ever been identified, nor did they never really understand the cause. All they knew was that corpses were wandering the world's streets hunting and eating humans alive. Whether recently dead or a one hundred year old crawling sack of bones with scarcely enough flesh to matter these beasts wanted food and humans were at the top of their menu.

Some people who had been attacked by zombies and had managed to survive with only scratches or bites usually ended up dying within a matter of days only to return to join the ever-multiplying ranks of the living dead.

Someone somewhere, no one recalled exactly who, discovered separating the zombies' heads from their bodies would kill them or perhaps re-kill them might be a better description. This temporarily gave the living humans a leg up so to speak on the slow moving and clumsy creatures. For a while, it seemed like the zombie threat would end by the efforts of the police, the armed forces and local. But eventually the walking dead won the day by the sheer overwhelming numbers.

When the authorities lost control of the situation, millions of distraught people chose to commit suicide rather than end up as a meal for the vile creatures. As a result, many of these suicides simply came back from the dead and became zombies themselves. The government eventually ordered all forms of burials to cease and proclaimed immediate cremation upon death would be the order of the day. They dug massive pits not only for the recently departed but for the remains of the zombies as well setting them ablaze with the hopes of keeping down the spread of disease.

However, when millions of rotting insect-riddled corpses walking about freely with sections of their skin sliding off, blood pooling in puddles everywhere and body parts rotting and falling to the ground the idea of disease control and sanitation became an impossibility. Once the utilities shut down and there was no more electricity, heat or clean water industrialized countries became something worse than third-world countries practically overnight. As a result, sickness ran rampant killing millions; further adding to the zombie population.

Now several months after "Zombie Ground Zero," the world of civilized humanity was essentially over with anarchy raging among survivors. A survivor was almost as likely to be killed by a fellow survivor as a walking cadaver. Some small pockets of humans still managed to stay alive by banding together in isolated areas, but it would only be a matter of time until they too would cease to be. Even if the zombies didn't get them, they might find themselves either dying of starvation, illness, or by being killed groups of other humans. Rumor had it some survivors had turned to cannibalism making them not much better than the roaming dead.

In an abandoned apartment in a small town in Schuylkill County, Pennsylvania Jonathan Bright opened he eyes to pitch blackness seeing night had fallen. Back in junior high more than a decade before the world had gone to Hell, some of the "over achievers" in his school gave Jonathan the dubious nickname "Notzo" as in "Not So Bright." He never minded the joke or the ribbing. He took over the name and actually sort of liked the attention, which went along with it. He was a quiet and reserved sort of person so being included made him feel a bit special. Before too long the nickname stuck and most of his friends knew him as Notzo although by now he suspected most, if not all, of those friends were gone.

Jonathan couldn't recall how long he had been sleeping this time; it might have been hours or it might have been days. Time didn't seem to have much relevance any longer in this repulsive new world. Now sitting in the darkness the last thing he recalled was a number of zombies had attacked him and somehow he had managed to escape finding his way into this building. He had no idea if he had been hurt and at the time didn't really care; he had been too exhausted to care so he just collapsed. How long ago that had been, he couldn't recall.

He lay on the floor deciding whether to bother waking up or to go back to sleep and try to regain his strength. He couldn't remember the last time he had eaten a meal and was famished. Food supplies were dwindling and unless something came in a can or unopened bottle survivors knew not to consume it.

Jonathan's thoughts were interrupted when he heard a rustling sound from somewhere in the room somewhere nearby. It was a sound, with which he had become frighteningly familiar. One or more of those walking carcasses was in the room with him. It sounded like two most likely bumbling about in their slow, spastic way. He heard them moaning and groaning making those guttural sounds they all seemed to make. He didn't know if it was some form of communication or just some left over living human memory telling them to try to speak. He knew if they found him here they would fall on him and rip his insides out, so he lay still, hoping they would simply give up and move on. He remembered his gun and carefully tried to feel around for it only to realize in his exhaustion, he must have dropped it somewhere in the room. There was little he could do now but to play dead and hope for the best.

After a few moments, he felt a bump against his ankle followed by a deep growl. He smelled the thing's decomposing flesh and realized, one of the creatures had just bumped into his leg. He was unsure what to do. For some odd reason the thing didn't yet recognize him as a human or else it would have attacked him immediately. He continued to lay still. Soon Jonathan heard more rustling nearby as he heard another one of the creatures approach to join the first. The two stood right next to him apparently confused about whether or not to attack. He found this extremely odd, as these savages never hesitated before. He had no previous understanding simply playing dead could fool the creatures but it seemed to be working for him so he continued to lie quietly, without a sound.

He recalled how someone had discovered the way to kill them by severing their brain stem. It was likely that fact had been accidently discovered as well. So maybe he was on to something here.

The second zombie struggled down to a kneeling position hovering just a few inches above Jonathan's face. On the verge of vomiting from the stench, combined with his fear and disgust, Jonathan forced himself to remain perfectly still. He decided if the thing got any closer he might have no choice but to try to roll away clear then fight his way out; better to go down with a fight than simply lie down and offer himself up as a main course. He chose to wait just a few moments longer. He wanted to see if he could pull off this playing possum idea.

The thing's pall of stench was beyond revolting as it hovered closer to Jonathan's face. Jonathan felt something fall from the creature landing on his own tightly closed lips. He could feel the thing crawling slowly across his lips its squirming body sliding and slithering. With utter revulsion, he realized a worm must have fallen from the monster's face and landed on his lips. These beasts had worms and maggots crawling in and out of their flesh constantly and now the tiny vermin was trying to find a way inside of his mouth. The slimy thing continued to writhe its way between Jonathan's tightly pursed lips.

After a few interminable moments of indecision, the two creatures miraculously gave up and lumbered away trudging across the room in their convulsive manner. The pair went out into the hall and stumbled down the stairs leaving the building. Jonathan listened for a few more moments, just long enough to be certain they were gone. The wait was excruciating. He could feel the maggot working its way between his lips. Once he was sure the coast was clear he spat out the vile creature struggled to his feet. Pain seemed to rack his body from head to toe. He assumed this pain was partially from a previous zombie attack he had survived and partially from lying on the hard floor for God knew how long.

Every muscle in his body was stiff as he clumsily staggered across the room closing the door to prevent any other zombies that might be lurking about from entering. He couldn't help but chuckle at how his awkward movements reminded him of the inept zombies, which had just left. "Bright of the living dead," he thought to himself amazed at somehow while his world was dying all around him he still managed to find humor in the oddest situations. Jonathan quietly closed the door and then latched the dead bolt.

"Dead bolt," Jonathan thought again chuckling; yet another one of those strange humor things but this time it sent a cold chill down his spine. Once he thought about it, he noticed he actually was quite cold. He would have to look around the room for a blanket or another coat.

Walking over to a boarded up window he did a quick glance outside through one of the cracks between the boards to see if any more of the creatures were out there and of course they were; since they were just about everywhere. He could see them staggering around in the moonlight. They seemed to walk about minding their own business oblivious to him standing inside the room just a few yards above them.

He reached into his pants pocket and took out a lighter flicking it to life and looking around his new surroundings. It appeared he was in a second floor bedroom of the building. Most of the furniture was gone. What little furniture remained was either lying scattered around the room or else broken into pieces. He found a decorative scented candle in a glass jar in one of the corners of the room. Using his lighter Jonathan lit the candle basking in the fragrant sweet scent of apple pie traveling up into his nose. It beat the hell out of the constant and interminable reek of decay that was the fragrance of the world these days. He realized he was going to have to find somewhere to get a bath sometime soon as he was becoming as ripe as those walking carcasses.

Continuing to investigate the room, Jonathan found a wooden chair seemed to be strong enough to support him and sat down to contemplate his next move. He also wanted to review the events, which led up to his being stuck in that room. He remembered running in the darkness through town in search of other survivors and trying to avoid the packs of man-hunting zombies. He had only let his guard down for a moment when three of the awful things had surrounded him. Pulling out his forty-five, he shot the first one right between the eyes, the creature's head exploding in rain of black blood, skull fragments and decayed brain matter.

One of the others had grabbed him snagging on the sleeve of his coat near the wrist. He had spun around and pistol-whipped the creature, shaking himself free just as the third one fell on his back trying to sink its rotten teeth into him and clawing uselessly at the leather jacket. Jonathan shook that last one off and ran down the alley for all he was worth. Although he couldn't remember exactly, he must have found this place and stumbled up to this room with his last ounce of strength before collapsing into unconsciousness.

Jonathan sat up straight with a jolt. His gun! Where was his gun? Holding the candle, he crawled on his hands and knees around the room looking for it until he noticed a glimmer of light reflecting in the candlelight. He saw the gun laying just a few feet from where he had slept. He was furious with himself not having it ready earlier when the two zombies were sniffing about the room. Then he realized it was probably best he hadn't found it because using it would have brought dozens more of the creatures down on his head.

Yet he still couldn't believe his luck or understand how he could have fooled them simply by pretending he was dead. Maybe these walking puss sacks were finally starting to lose it. Maybe their rotting brains were winding down, and they would eventually simply die off; perhaps not. He wondered what would happen when there wasn't enough of the living remaining to sustain the dead. Perhaps they'd just sit down and rot away to nothing, turning the future of the earth over to the insects and animals once again.

Jonathan suddenly got an idea, although a slightly crazy and potentially dangerous idea. If he could fool the zombies once, perhaps he could fool them again. Now that he thought about it every time he or anyone else encountered the walking dead, they did what any sane human would do; they either ran away screaming or attacked and tried to kill the things. As such, the zombies had reacted in kind. He couldn't remember a single instance where someone had pretended to be dead or pretended to be one of the zombies to see what would happen. Mankind was simply not made that way; the fight or flight instinct was just too strong.

Jonathan wondered what would happen, if instead of acting like a typical human, he acted like one of them. He imagined himself lumbering down the street acting exactly like one of the living dead dragging his leg and moaning mournfully. It sounded absolutely crazy at first, but the more he thought about it the more he liked it. After all, he had sort of proven the theory just a little while earlier. The two zombies, which had him pinned helpless in the room didn't attack him. Jonathan assumed it had been because they thought he was already dead. The he considered another problem, pretending he was dead lying on a floor was one thing but pretending he was one of them walking around among them might be a whole other thing entirely. He was excited about the possibility and had to test it to see if it would work; and somehow he believed it would.

Jonathan decided he'd wait until daylight. Then he'd watch until there were only one or two of them walking around outside and he'd put his gun in his jacket pocket just in case. Next, he planned to stagger out into the street; out among them shuffling like the zombies did and would see how they reacted. It they ignored them he'd continue walking. If they tried to attack him, he'd simply blow their heads off and run back to safety before any others saw him. It was good he had to wait a while because at that moment, his muscles were really aching and stiff. He guessed it might be a few hours until daylight and if he stayed awake and took time to stretch a bit the aches would eventually go away.

He was eager to test out his new idea because he was quite literally starving. He hadn't eaten for days, and if this new strategy worked, it would give him a lot more freedom to move around among the accursed things without consequence.

For several hours, he stood; paced and walked around the room bending and stretching from time to time trying to get that stiffness out of his muscles but didn't seem to have much luck. He needed to get outside, out of the dismal room, out into the world to move around. Then he might be able to find some food.

Jonathan saw the morning sun shining through the slits between the boards covering the window on the east side of the room. He walked over to the window and carefully removed one of the boards from the lower corner of the window frame and looked outside. There didn't seem to be any zombie activity in the area.

He quietly walked over to the locked door, placing his ear against it and listening for any movement in the upstairs hall. He knew if they were out there he'd hear them because they were mindless, reanimated lumps of what was once human flesh. They were completely void of any intelligence or the ability to plan and strategize. It wasn't as if they could lie quietly in the darkness waiting for him to give up and come out. That was simply not, how they functioned. They could no more suppress their noises than could a hurricane. Jonathan suspected they didn't even think when attacking, being driven by some internal instinct or hunger rather than any form of logical thought.

Jonathan unlatched the deadbolt then slowly turned the doorknob keeping his shoulder against the door in case he had to close it quickly. He opened the door about two inches, half expecting to see several living dead fingers push their way through the gap but nothing happened.

He pulled the door open hesitated for a moment trying his best to remember the types of spastic movements these creatures made then he staggered out into the upstairs hall. He forced a dull and slack look onto his face. Unfortunately, he couldn't duplicate the gray film of death, which covered the zombie's eyes but if he kept his head down and avoided eye contact, he still might be all right.

He slowly turned his head to the left and right looking down the hall, watching and listening for any zombies but found none. Continuing in his awkward gate he made his way to the top of the stairs again looking and listening. Little by little, one single step at a time Jonathan made his way down the long flight of stairs stopping occasionally when a particular step would let out an extra loud creak. He thought to himself if this plan worked out, he'd have to remember for future reference not to be so cautious walking around. That was a human trait; the zombies always stumbled about knocking down whatever was in their way without consideration. But for now he decided caution would still be the best way to handle this experiment; until he was out among them. Again, he thought of his "Bright of the Living Dead" comment earlier and had to suppress a nervous chuckle.

When he found himself at the bottom of the stairs, he saw there was only a ten-foot hall separating him from the outside world. The front door stood open as so many doors did these days. He could see out into the street in front of the building as a cool late March breeze blew in on him. He had forgotten to look for a coat in the room and as a result, he was still very cold. What he found odd was the fact he wasn't shivering. Jonathan was one of those people who would shiver at the drop of a hat, but now he was colder than he had been in a long time yet wasn't shivering. Perhaps that was a good thing, he thought. Because if a zombie saw him shaking with cold, that might blow his cover.

As he trudged down the hall he practiced his "zombie" walking doing his best to replicate their clumsy gate always keeping his hand inside his jacket pocket on the handle of his gun. When he got about three feet from the doorway, a zombie shuffled into view out on the street stopping right in front of the opening staring directly at Jonathan. The beast was no more than fifteen feet away. A lump of apprehension arose in Jonathan's throat and for a moment, he almost gave up. The front door was only a foot or two beyond his reach now, and he knew he could easily grab it and slam it shut before the creature got to him, but he was determined to see if his idea would work.

He kept his head down continuing to drag his way toward the doorway looking upward under his turned down brow to see what the creature was doing. Sure enough, the zombie looked the other way with complete disinterest and continued on its way. Jonathan couldn't believe his luck. This truly was as important a discovery as learning about shooting them in the head. As soon as he found some survivors, he'd make certain he passed the word. Now that he thought about it, this trick could mean the salvation of all mankind.

He stepped down onto the street and still keeping his head cast downward, he could see there were many of them, perhaps ten or twenty wandering about aimlessly. Jonathan recalled how when they weren't busy eating someone these creatures could be almost comical to watch as the milled about imitating things they once did when alive. He remembered one time seeing a female zombie in a filthy torn tennis outfit slowly swinging a broken racket into empty air. The frayed racket face had strings missing and those few remaining were hanging in complete disarray. He recalled a zombie soldier sitting on the side of a curb with one hand holding his rifle saluting at no one in particular.

After walking for a time Jonathan noticed he was in what once was the downtown shopping area surrounded by the living dead roaming in and out of burned out businesses. He made his way onto the pavement noting a grocery store not too far away on the corner. If he could get inside, he might be able to find something to eat or drink without the creatures noticing.

Suddenly a high-pitched scream interrupted Jonathan's thoughts. He looked up to see a young woman, a living human survivor standing about ten feet in front of him panting, drenched with sweat and out of breath. She must have come around the corner stumbling onto his street by mistake while being pursued by other zombies and suddenly realized she was really in big trouble. Jonathan lifted his head and as his eyes met hers he never felt so helpless in his life. Already the zombies were had started to surround her, their moaning increasing. He tried to speak quietly to tell her to run but when he attempted to speak nothing came out but a crackly groan.

"Damn!" he thought to himself. He hadn't had anything to drink for hours and his throat must be too dry to speak.

Again, she screamed helplessly staring right at him as the zombies closed in on her. He didn't know what he should do. It was too late to try to help her escape. His experiment had worked perhaps too well. He and the girl were in the middle of at least twenty zombies, surrounding her and they still didn't recognize he wasn't one of them. There was no way he could shoot his way out of the situation with his pistol and if he blew his cover, he'd likely die along with the woman.

"Survival of the fittest" he thought to himself and put his head down as the zombies fell upon the woman first ripping out her stomach and intestines then eventually ripping her limb from limb in a savage feeding frenzy.

Jonathan stood staring at the spectacle unable to move. After a few seconds, he felt a bump against his legs and noticed the woman's hand must have been thrown in the struggle for food and had landed right at his feet. He stood staring at the severed limb dumbfounded, in shock. Then he saw the blood pooling under the hand, and he suddenly noticed how pink and warm the flesh of the hand looked. For the first time since he had awoken in that apartment, he felt a rush of warmth climbing through his body. Then he actually felt a growing savage hunger telling him he should bend down lick the flesh and taste the blood of the severed limb.

Jonathan thought he must be losing his mind, going insane with hunger. In disgust, he turned away and found himself staring at a zombie version of himself in the glass door of the grocery store. Slowly he staggered toward the door mouth agape, as the image grew larger and clearer. He raised his arms leaning them against the glass placing his face against the reflection. His eyes were no longer sharp and focused but were covered in a gray cataract-like film of death. He lifted his head away from the glass and noticed his jacket sleeve had slid down revealing a large maggot riddled wound on his lower right arm caked with dried blood.

He thought back to the night before when one of his zombie attackers had grabbed the sleeve of his jacket. The thing must have cut and infected him. Perhaps the days of sleeping had allowed the infection to spread. Jonathan understood now he hadn't really been fooling the zombies; he had been fooling himself. He was becoming one of them, and the transformation was almost complete.

He looked back at the severed hand looking beautiful, pink and delicious in the morning sunlight and felt his thoughts start to slip away as a red fire of hunger began to take their place. The last human thought he had before his mind slipped completely away was "Bright of the Living Dead," but it didn't seem so funny anymore.

BREAKFAST OF CHAMPIONS

Ray loved breakfast. It was by far his favorite meal of the day. And whenever eating breakfast there was nothing Ray loved better than a heaping plateful of scrambled eggs, hash browns (or home fries in a pinch), buttered toast, a cup of steaming tea with cream and sugar and most notably bacon.

To Ray Johnson there was nothing so important for bringing out the taste of a great breakfast than a delicious double serving of good old-fashioned bacon. Not the cheap thin fatty store-brand garbage his wife tried to pass off on him sometimes but the good stuff; the bacon, which had a much larger meat to fat ratio than you could find at most grocery stores. He preferred the kind of bacon you could only find in an authentic butcher shop.

In the mind of Raymond J. Johnson, Jr. there was nothing comparable to the taste of bacon. Yes, he had been given the dubious name Raymond J. Johnson, Junior. His father, Ray Sr. had been a huge fan of the 1970's light beer commercials featuring comedian Bill Saluga, who did a shtick featuring a character known as Raymond Jay Johnson Jr. In the act, Bill would ramble on incessantly saying things like, "My name is Raymond Jay Johnson Jr., but you doesn't have to call me Mr. Johnson. You can call me Ray, or you can call me Jay, or you can call me . . ." This would go on and on until at some point it would mercifully end with him saying, "But you doesn't have to call me Mr. Johnson."

It was one of those commercial catch phrases like "Where's the beef?" and for some strange reason, Ray Sr. loved it. Since his name was Raymond J. (for John)

Johnson he often had fun at work walking around the office repeating Saluga's monolog. He was sorry he wasn't a junior; that would have made it perfect.

He told his wife, "If we ever have a son, we're going to call him Raymond J. Johnson Jr. A boy could have lots of fun with a name like that." By the time Ray Jr. was born and eventually had grown to the age where he might "enjoy" the name, the world had moved on and most people didn't recall the commercials. From time to time some "remember when" type of special might show a clip of Bill Saluga's act and Ray Jr. would take some ribbing at school the next day, but it never lasted, a fact for which he was grateful.

Silly name aside one thing Ray did inherit from both of his parents was good genes. At fifty years old, Ray never exercised except for yard work on the weekends, was only slightly overweight, had low cholesterol and perfect blood pressure. When one of your favorite pastimes was eating fried eggs, potatoes and meat for breakfast this little physical benefit came in very handy.

Often Ray would go out to breakfast with his health nut co-workers who would sit picking at fruit and non-fat yogurt and other forms of heart-friendly food terrified even a single bite of fat or one drop of grease would instantly stop their tickers. All the while Ray would be gulping down a plateful of scrambled eggs fried in butter, hash brown fried potatoes, still glistening with grease and of course a mountain of fried bacon. His coworkers would look on in amazement, warning him he was killing himself and would probably be dead by the age of fifty-five. Ray would simply laugh and tell them, "Boys, this is what I call the breakfast of champions." Then he would go back to gulping down his meal with a euphoric look of pleasure.

Ray often traveled for business and whenever possible made a point of scheduling his trips so he would arrive at his destination the night before his appointment. That way he could check around and find the best place for breakfast in the area. He always tried to avoid the fast-food chains and larger concerns and looked deliberately for the out of the way, "Mom and Pop" breakfast nooks, where he was virtually guaranteed to get a really good, special and unique breakfast. And every time he would wait with anticipation for their bacon. There were times he was disappointed with a particular establishment but for the most part, he was usually satisfied. Sometimes he'd get really lucky and find an out of the way place with incredible breakfast and outstanding bacon.

That was why he found himself in Bart's Forge, West Virginia at 7:00 am standing in front of what looked like a very promising place for breakfast. The restaurant was at the edge of town, housed in what may have once been a large barn, which seemed to back up against a farm. The hotel desk clerk told him this was the best place for breakfast in the entire county. The restaurant apparently opened at 5:00 am and was only open for breakfast, no longer taking any orders past 10:00 am.

The place had a very interesting name, "Bob's Bacon Barn." Now that Ray was actually standing in front of the place he found himself looking on in awe at the name, displayed boldly in neon high above the entrance. Not only did Ray feel the name was creative but the name was displayed in a font, resembling strips of bacon, twisted and formed into letters.

"Oh my sweet Lord in Heaven!" Ray said. He appeared to be in a state of rapture usually reserved for people experiencing a religious epiphany. But for Raymond J. Johnson, Jr. this was his religion, his nirvana.

He just knew this place had to have what might turn out to be the greatest breakfast he had ever eaten. "This will be one for the record books," he said as he used his cell phone camera to take a quick shot of the front of the place. Yes, Ray did have a scrapbook of his favorite breakfast haunts from all around the country and was certain Bob's Bacon Barn would deserve a special place in the book. It wasn't like Ray to make such an assumption, but something about the place told him he was right.

His first appointment was about twenty miles away and wasn't until 9:00 am so he had plenty of time to relax and enjoy one of his greatest pleasures in life, breakfast. Ray walked through the large glass front door, which was housed inside of what at one time was one of two large barn doors.

"Cool!" Ray thought to himself, "What a great idea keeping the barn appearance but adding a modern door."

As he opened the door, one of the most scrumptious smells he had ever experienced hit his olfactory senses and he feared he might start drooling from the amazing aroma of the wonderful restaurant.

Ray seemed to float as in a dream in the restaurant past the sign reading "Please Park Your Own Pork" mounted on a large cartoon character resembling Porky Pig instructing regulars to seat themselves. The luscious smells of the place were unbelievable and Ray took in every single glorious aroma as he floated to the nearest available table. He wasn't surprised to find locating an empty table was difficult. Any place, which smelled this good was bound to have a packed house day after day.

He looked around the large room and saw the place had once been an actual barn. It was decorated in rustic wood and timber and had a two story peaked ceiling from which hung a bright assortment of larger plastic pink pigs adorned with angel wings. A large ceiling fan hung from the center of the ceiling turning slowly generating just enough air current to keep the pigs in motion, appearing to fly high above the crowds below.

Ray could tell a large percentage of the people in the restaurant were locals by the way they all seemed to know each other and were all engaged in animated conversations, but there were a few people who stood out as possibly business people or tourists.

A waitress dressed is a 1950's style uniform with the name "Aggie" embroidered above the left pocket approached Ray's table with a menu and introduced herself as his server. She asked if he wanted to see a menu, which had an assortment of bacon-related breakfast choices. Ray declined, as he knew exactly what he liked and he always ordered the exact same thing.

"No, thank you." Ray replied. "Just bring me three scrambled eggs, hash browns, if you have 'em, some buttered toast and a heapin' helpin' of your finest bacon."

Aggie set the menu on the table then started to write his order on her order pad. Ray inquired, "This is a really interesting place. Is the bacon really as good as I hope it's going to be?"

"Yes sir," Aggie replied. "Not only will it meet your expectations, but it'll surpass them. I can guarantee it. You see, Bob owns this restaurant as well as his own hog farm, slaughterhouse and butcher business. He supplies meat for restaurants all over the state. But he keeps the very special bacon reserved for this place right here. It's the only place anywhere that you can get Bob's special home blend of bacon. That's why people come from all around the state to enjoy breakfast with Bob."

"Wow!" Ray said. "I can't wait to try it."

"Would you like some coffee while you're waiting?" Aggie asked.

"If it wouldn't be too much trouble could you bring me a cup of tea with cream and three sugars?"

Aggie replied, "One cup of hot tea with cream and three sugars coming right up Darlin'. I'll be back in two shakes and your breakfast should be up in a few minutes."

The waitress left Ray sitting in anticipation of the arrival of what showed promise of being the best breakfast he had ever eaten. Ray looked down at the laminated menu resting on the red and white-checkered tablecloth. He figured why not pass the time by checking out what else the place had to offer. The menu had the same Bob's Bacon Barn logo across the top with a cartoon pig wearing a straw hat grinning and pointing at the logo. It listed a variety of breakfast creations all of which featured bacon and any one of which could have satisfied Ray such as bacon wraps, bacon croissants, bacon sandwiches and other such items. However, whenever he ate at a restaurant for the first time, Ray always ordered the exact same combination. He felt this way when he was weighing one place against those he had visited in the past he could do an "apples to apples" type of comparison, or perhaps "bacon to bacon" would be a more appropriate statement. He figured, if he came back here the next day he could get creative and order one of the other options.

Aggie arrived back with his tea. "Here you go, sir. I certainly hope you enjoy your morning tea."

"I'm sure I will," Ray replied. Then he inquired, "Does, Mister, I mean, does Bob ever stop by the restaurant to meet the customers?"

Aggie said, "Bob, his name is actually Bob Evans, no relation to the national restaurant chain, does make a point of stopping by whenever he can to make sure things are running smoothly and everyone is getting their money's worth. I'm not sure if he'll be stopping by this morning. I guess we'll just have to wait and see." Then she turned and headed to the next table.

About three minutes later Aggie returned with Ray's breakfast. It was a remarkable sight, which for Ray was beyond comprehension. An enormous mountain of scrambled eggs adorned his plate, obviously fried in real butter. In addition, there was a heap of golden hash browns as well as four slices of toast glistening with more butter. On the side was a gigantic pile of the best-looking bacon he had ever seen. Each slice appeared to be over an eighth of an inch thick, at least ninety-five percent meat with only a slight bit of fat marbling the bacon in just the right way. The aroma emanating up from the plate was in Ray's opinion pure ecstasy. For the first time in his life, Raymond J. Johnson Jr. actually felt guilty eating such an amazing sight. He thought it belonged on the cover of some glossy food magazine.

Nonetheless, Ray did what he did best and plunged headlong into his breakfast. As he ate the amazing feast, his brain filled with all sorts of images, as his senses seemed to go temporarily mad with delight. A few times during his feeding frenzy, Aggie stopped by to see if he needed anything, but Ray seemed not to hear her as he was in another place, a place of pure savory delight.

When he had finally finished, Ray appeared to wake up from a dream as he stared disapprovingly at his empty plate. He wasn't ready for the experience to be over and wanted more of that incredible flavor but at the same time, he sensed he was extremely full. He was sure if he ate another bite he would end up making himself sick. What a quandary he was experiencing! His taste buds craved more but his body was telling him he had already eaten too much. Slowly he forced himself to back away from the table and take a much-needed deep breath.

It was as Ray had predicted, the most scrumptious breakfast he had ever experienced. With a slight bit of melancholy, he realized if he lived to be one hundred and ate breakfast every day for the rest of his life he'd never find a breakfast as good as this one.

For a moment, he had the flash of an idea that maybe he would move his family out here to Bart's Forge so he could experience this breakfast every day from now on. Then with a bit of sadness he realized there was no way his wife would be willing to move to a place, which obviously offered very little in economic opportunity, not simply so he could have his favorite breakfast. She'd likely divorce him first. For a moment, he actually even considered divorce as a viable option.

Then realized the answer was still no. For Raymond J. Johnson Jr., when this business trip was over he would have to go back to eating breakfasts he knew would never compare with the one he just ate. Perhaps whenever possible he could arrange to have business trips to this area of the country and could make a point of stopping by Bob's Bacon Barn often. Yes, that was what he'd do. He'd even wake up early and travel an hour for this experience again if necessary. He chuckled to himself when he realized his new-found love affair with Bob's Bacon Barn wasn't all that different than if he had found a woman in the town and he had to sneak back to see her.

"Sir?" Ray heard a voice calling him from nearby, awakening him from his gastronomically induced trance.

"Sir? Is everything all right? Did you enjoy your breakfast?"

"Aggie, that was by far the most incredible breakfast I've ever eaten in my entire life."

Aggie said, "Earlier you had mentioned wanting to meet Bob, Mr. Evans the owner of the restaurant. He just arrived in the building, and if you'd like I'd be happy to tell him you want to say hello."

Ray was thrilled with excitement, "Please Aggie, by all means ask Mr. Evans if he'd be kind enough to stop by. I'd love to compliment him on this amazing feast."

A few moments later Aggie approached the table with a tall rotund man in a pair of jeans and a flannel shirt. She said, "Mr. Evans, this is the man I was telling you about. He just loves your bacon."

The large man reached out a huge paw of a hand and said, "Bob Evans, proprietor of this fine establishment. I'm happy to make your acquaintance."

Ray stood and extended his own hand and said, "Raymond J. Johnson, Jr., please have a seat."

Evans sat down across the table from Ray and said with a sly smile, "I suppose I doesn't has to call you Johnson, but I can call you Ray or I can call you Jay . . ." Then he winked at Ray. Obviously, Bob Evans who probably took a lot of ribbing for his own name appreciated what Ray must have gone through growing up with a name like that.

"I see you're familiar with the routine," Ray replied.

"Yes. I feel your pain."

The two seemed to strike up an instant friendship and after several minutes of Ray praising the quality of the food he decided to take a bold step and asked, "Bob, I've never actually seen how bacon is, shall we say, processed. I'm so amazed with the quality of your bacon I'd consider it an honor if you would show me where and how all of this takes place."

Evans seemed to think about it for a moment, and then he looked at Ray as if he was appraising a prize hog and said, "Well, I usually don't let too many folks in on my secrets, especially when it comes to my bacon. But you seem like the sort of fella who truly appreciates a good breakfast, so I guess I can make an exception for you. Say, you're not from around these parts are you?"

Ray replied, "No, sir. I'm a businessman from a little town in Schuylkill County Pennsylvania called Ashton not a whole lot bigger than your little town just a lot hillier. So you know I appreciate fine food like you serve right here in Bart's Forge."

"Well then, that being said, why don't you stop back here around one this afternoon, and I'll give you a private tour of my hog farm and my slaughterhouse."

For a moment, hearing the man say the word "slaughterhouse" and seeing a strange gleam of happiness appear in the man's eye, Ray felt a strange chill creep down his spine and his stomach seemed to tighten just slightly. Perhaps some primitive instinct was warning him something might not be right.

Putting the strange feeling out of his mind, Ray replied with some trepidation, "Sure thing, Bob. I'll be happy to stop back at one."

Evans must have noticed the slight hesitation in his voice, "Not to worry, Ray. I sense you might be a bit uncomfortable with the slaughterhouse part of the tour, but I guarantee you it's not as bad as you might think. And I'll tell you what. If you feel in any way uneasy when we're in the slaughterhouse, we'll end the tour and send you on your way. But if you want to see the real secret behind the best tasting bacon in the state if not the country you'll want to see everything."

"Very well then, I'll see you back here at one."

The two men shook hands, and Ray watched the large man work his way around the restaurant shaking hands with the various customers. Ray mentally scolded himself for his momentary uneasiness. He realized he had nothing to worry about. It wasn't like this fellow was some sort of psycho like that crazy couple from the movie "Motel Hell" who ground up people to make their prize sausage or anything like that. He was simply a hard working entrepreneur who produced the best bacon Ray had ever tasted.

Ray settled his bill and headed toward the front door. As he approached the door, he noticed something he must have missed on the way in. Off to the side of the door was a massive stuffed hog. It was the largest hog Ray had ever seen, not that he had a lot of experience with hogs. He had however, been to the Pennsylvania Farm Show several times and had seen a good many prize hogs. This creature, however, was twice as big as any he had ever seen. It was mounted on a platform with a background depicting a farm scene. There was a sign at the base of the stand, which read, "Nelly - Prize Hog and Beloved Pet."

Ray thought to himself if the rest of Bob's hogs were this huge it was no wonder why he was so successful and why his bacon was so incredible. Ray left the restaurant and headed to his appointment relaxed with a full stomach and an anticipation of his tour with Evans in the afternoon.

Promptly at 1:00PM, Ray returned to the restaurant to find it closed for the day. He walked to the front door and shielding his eyes from the sun peered in to see if anyone was still inside, but it was empty.

He slowly walked around to the side of the restaurant and heard some activity coming from another barn located behind the restaurant. Ray approached the open door of the barn and saw Bob Evans dressed now in a tee shirt and coveralls feeding some of his pigs, which were rapidly devouring the slop in their troughs. Ray was amazed at how well built the man was with muscles bulging from the sleeves of his shirt. At first appearance Ray thought the man fat and out of shape, but now he realized, although very much overweight, the man was still very strong and muscular.

"Hello?" Ray called, "Bob? Mr. Evans? It's me Ray Johnson." Ray could smell the pungent stench of the live hogs.

Evans stopped what he was doing and walked toward Ray wiping his hands on his coveralls then reaching out to shake Ray's hand. "Glad you could stop by, Ray. If you'll give me a few minutes to finish slopping these hogs, we can begin our tour."

Ray asked, "Are these the hogs you use to make your delicious bacon?"

Evans replied in surprise, "What? These puny things? Heavens no! I'll slaughter these hogs in a few weeks after I fatten them up a bit. They'll be processed and sent out to the various stores in the area. Granted they'll still produce some of the finest bacon, chops and pork roast in the state, but they're nowhere near the quality of what you ate this morning. The hogs used to produce that bacon are much larger and receive very special care and feeding."

This reminded Ray of something he saw that morning, "That hog in the front of your restaurant had to be the largest such creature I've ever seen. Will the hogs we will be seeing that huge?"

Evans stopped for a second looking like he had been struck, then he caught himself and continued, "Uh yes. They'll be more in line with Nelly you saw in the barn. She was my first hog of her type. She was the one I used to test out my special recipe feed. In fact, every one of the hogs used in the production of my prize-winning bacon is a direct descendant of Nelly. As you could see, I could never slaughter her. She was more like a pet, hell almost like family. When she passed on I chose to have her mounted and displayed forever in the restaurant."

Evans continued with his chores and when finished said proudly, "Alright, Ray. Let's go back to the next building, and I'll show you the hogs that make the best bacon in the state."

The two men walked back through the long barn and out a pair of double doors across a long yard to another much larger barn hidden from street view.

"Now you'd better prepare yourself, Raymond. These babies are at least as large as Nelly, a few maybe even bigger."

Although Ray thought he would be prepared for what he'd see, he soon discovered he wasn't. As they entered the barn, Ray saw immediately the hogs in this area were at least two feet taller than the enormous stuffed Nelly. They were also several feet longer and much wider.

Unlike the smaller pigs in the first barn, there were no wooden fences keeping them penned inside, but instead Ray saw open top cages made out of what appeared to be two-inch thick solid steel bars. The beast in the cage closest to them sniffed the air and started to salivate madly. The menacing creature charged headlong into the bars and was knocked back just as quickly by a jolt of electricity. Shaking its head dazed from the voltage, the beast howled in pain.

"You don't want to get too close to those bars," Evans said. "There's enough juice going through them to fry you ten times over. I know it's dangerous, but the electricity and the cages are the only way I have to keep them contained."

"Oh my Lord!" Ray exclaimed. "How in the name of Heaven did you ever manage to grow them so big."

"Well, many, many years ago, back when Nelly was a piglet, I started to work on a variety of feeds to help the pigs grow larger but at the same time leaner. I'm sure you noticed the perfect marbling of minimal fat and the abundance of meat in your bacon this morning. The special feed I developed requires some ingredients, which are often difficult to come by so I only feed it to a few select hogs, which I eventually butcher and use for the bacon I serve at the restaurant. The rest of the hogs on the farm get traditional feed and as a result, I sell them for general use. As I said, all of my meat is excellent but the meat from these fine specimens is by far the greatest."

"But the size of them! You must be using some type of steroid or something to cause their enormous size."

"Absolutely not!" Evans insisted. "These hogs are raised on one hundred percent natural feed and their size is gained through careful and selective breeding."

Ray asked, "So tell me about this feed. What is it about this feed that's so special?"

"Well come on back to the slaughterhouse, and I'll be happy to show you."

The two walked slowly through the barn. All the while, the hogs growled and drooled wanting to break out and devour them. Soon Ray found himself in another huge building, obviously the slaughterhouse. The smell of blood and death were overpowering. For a moment, he thought he might vomit but managed to suppress the feeling.

"See?" Evans continued, "It's not so bad in here. After a while, the smell tends to grow on you. I'll tell you what. See that steel dumpster over there?"

Ray looked over and saw a huge shiny steel dumpster on hinges attached to what appeared to be a giant meat grinder.

Evans explained, "In there is the secret ingredients for my special brand of hog feed. Go ahead, take a look."

Ray walked slowly to the dumpster and peered over the side. What he saw made him freeze in terror. The dumpster was filled with human body parts. A horrid assortment of dismembered arms, legs, hands and severed heads both male and female filled the bin. Flies and maggots crawled in and out of the mouths of the severed heads. An incredible stench rose up from the pile of human debris, causing Ray's stomach to turn over once again.

"What the Hell!" Ray shouted just before he felt the felt a jolt of electricity at the back of his neck and the world went black. That phrase would be the last sentence Raymond J. Johnson Jr. would ever have a chance to utter.

Sometime later, Ray began to regain consciousness finding himself gagged and strapped to a filthy wooden table unable to move. Across the room, he saw Bob Evans slowly walking arm in arm with Aggie the waitress from the restaurant. She was carrying something in her right arm, which appeared to Ray to be a chainsaw.

"We're going to do you a favor, Ray old boy." Evans said, "Today you had the opportunity to taste the best breakfast in the world, and let's be honest here. From now on, nothing else you'd ever eat could possibly be able to compare. So rather than have you spend the rest of your life miserably trying in vain to find one equal we're going to end your misery right here and now. Think of it this way, Ray; you're providing a service helping others enjoy the pleasure you enjoyed today."

Ray heard Aggie starting the chain saw and mercifully fell into unconsciousness brought on by the searing pain as she began to dismember him alive, one limb at a time.

THE LURKERS

The hall light never seemed to be bright enough. Tommy watched it dimly glowing behind its yellowed bowl-shaped glass globe. He had become very familiar with its raised floral pattern having stood staring at it many times in his past ten years of life.

The meager ceiling light located at the top of the stairs was meant to provide sufficient illumination not only for the stairway but for the long frightening hallway appearing to go on forever like a horrifying tunnel of unknown terrors.

The hall led to an open door at its darkest end; Tommy's bedroom. His door was always open; he never closed it. He suspected someday he might want it closed for privacy but not for the moment. Right now privacy was the last thing he wanted to think about.

Presently he wanted people around him, lots of people the more the merrier; anything but finding himself alone with that dreadful hall positioned between him and the sanctuary of his bedroom. It loomed before him like a passageway to unimaginable horrors. Perhaps unimaginable wasn't the right word because Tommy could imagine the horrors. In fact, he could imagine things much more horrifying than most people would ever envision. And when he thought hard enough about these imaginings they seemed to be completely real; and perhaps on some level they were.

Tommy could see his doorway waiting at the end of the hall like a beckoning safe haven. All he had to do was make it to his room then he could jump into his bed pull the covers up over his head and they couldn't get him; those beings, the ones he called The Lurkers.

He stood with his back against the wall at the top of the stairs looking down at the light shining into the stairwell from the living room. He could hear the sounds of his parents and older sisters who were watching *My Three Sons* on their black and white Philco TV. He could hear the crotchety voice of Uncle Charlie complaining about something or other as always. Tommy recalled Uncle Charlie was a fairly new character to the show, having replaced the boy's grandfather, Bub O'Casey who Tommy overheard his Dad say was sick or too old or something. Although he liked the grandfather character, Uncle Charlie seemed to be pretty cool as well. That was, on those rare occasions when he was allowed to stay up to watch the show. The comforting sounds of the TV helped to relax his pounding heart at least for the moment.

To Tommy's left, his parents' bedroom was visible through the open doorway; the glow from a nearby streetlight shown across the bed. Tommy never was afraid of this room no matter how dark because it was his mom and dad's room, and the Lurkers would never go in there.

He turned his head slowly to the right looking down the dark menacing hallway. The right side of the hall was what he thought of as the "safe zone." His family lived in the end unit of a row home and the right side of the hall was attached to the house next door so there was nowhere for them to hide along that wall. Often he would creep along the right side with his back pressed firmly against the wall and his eyes squeezed tightly shut.

The left side of the hall was a completely different story; that was where all the trouble was. Along the left side were two doorways. The first led to his older sisters' bedroom and the last, which was adjacent to his bedroom, was for the family bathroom. Although he knew they could lurk in either room, for some reason the bathroom was the most frightening. Perhaps because it also had a huge cast iron bathtub, the one with four scary feet looking like those of an eagle. Often during the light of day when Tommy was using the toilet, he would imagine those huge clawed feet moving, just a slight bit. He wondered if the tub might someday creep slowly toward him like a lumbering dinosaur and crush him while he did his business.

Tommy parents called his fears "irrational," Although he wasn't quite sure what irrational meant he suspected it meant he was letting his imagination run away with him again. They always told him he had a tendency to do that. Whatever the meaning he knew irrational or not The Lurkers were as real to him as the sweat beading on his forehead right now.

It was strange how Tommy's fears worked. If it was daytime or someone else was in one of the rooms, Tommy was fine because he knew The Lurkers only wanted him. The things lurking in the rooms didn't want anyone else and wouldn't come around if anyone else was present.

Tommy wasn't sure exactly what it was lurking behind those doorways at night or why they had chosen him. All he could ever see was blackness, but what he could imagine was much, much worse. He never imagined clowns, werewolves, vampires or any of the typical things other kids his age feared. No, Tommy's imaginings were much more frightening than anything so simple.

The creatures he imagined had no real name he was aware of other than "The Lurkers" because he had given them that name. This was because of the way they lurked in the darkness always watching, always waiting. He feared these creatures more than anything. In his imagination, Tommy saw these creatures as thin, grayish-skinned beings who he envisioned occasionally looking out around the door frames at him down the dark hall with their long slimy fingers and dark black eyes with blood red pupils staring eagerly at him. Tommy didn't know what they wanted with him, but he was certain it wasn't friendship. He suspected if he walked by a doorway where one of the things was waiting they might simply reach out their wet hands and gently brush his cheek. He knew if he felt their horrible snake-like skin against his own flesh his heart might stop from fear, and his parents would find him dead on the hall floor.

Tonight, like every other night he had to go to bed before everyone else, Tommy found himself trembling in fear at the slow and frightening journey he had to take in order to get to his room. But tonight Tommy hoped things might be a little different. Tonight he had something to help him battle his fear and perhaps make it, and those horrible Lurkers disappear forever.

Tommy's Sunday school teacher Mrs. Fleisher had presented a special class where she talked about fears young people have, such as fear of the dark, fear of heights and things like that. Tommy listened to her intently recalling her saying if he ever felt afraid, all he had to do is repeat the phrase, "There's nothing to be afraid of. God's always with me," and whatever his fear he could defeat it with the power of God Almighty. Tonight that phrase had become a mantra to Tommy, one he repeated in a whisper continuously as he prepared to face his most dreaded fears and venture down the horrible corridor, past the lurking creatures.

"Are you in bed yet?" the stern voice of his father called up from downstairs interrupting his mental repetitions. Tommy covered his mouth with his hand to make his voice sound muffled and far away then replied, "Yes, Dad, I'm in bed. Goodnight." His father shouted, "You better be. Because if you're up there in the hall crying again, I'll come up and give you something to cry about." He heard his sisters giggling in the background.

"Oh, George! Leave him alone!" he heard his mother admonish. His mom seemed to understand his fear no matter how irrational it might seem, and this was a fact for which Tommy was extremely grateful. Perhaps he had gotten his active imagination from his mother and that was why she understood; he didn't know but was nonetheless thankful.

There had been many nights, when Tommy would deliberately refuse to go upstairs to his room alone and would "act up" just so his father would get angry and chase him up the stairs and down the hall to his room. Even though Tommy knew a sharp whack on the backside awaited him when his father caught him, it was a thousand times better than facing the lurking things in the hall. Luckily, his father wasn't the abusive type so the sore backside he would receive would often go away within a few minutes. His dad was just a typical dad of the nineteen sixty's and wasn't opposed to giving occasional spankings. Tommy figured a few minutes with a stinging backside was much better than walking down that horrible hall alone.

But tonight he was determined to face his fear head on armed with his new special phrase. Tommy was sure with the power of God himself no lurking thing could ever harm him. Tommy stepped tentatively away from the wall and keeping his hands by his side, he turned to his right. Now focusing his eyes on his bedroom doorway, he started walking slowly down the center of the hall.

In his mind he began reciting, "There's nothing to be afraid of. God's always with me." He repeated this with his lips moving in cadence with his thoughts. With each frightening step, he said his powerful phrase confident no evil thing would be able to touch him. Eyes still focused on his bedroom after about five steps he estimated he was passing his sisters' bedroom doorway. He squeezed his eyes shut, as he didn't want to see any creatures looking out at him. Even if his newfound power prevented The Lurkers from getting him, he still didn't want to see them. He had never seen them anywhere but in his mind and didn't want to start tonight. That he could certainly do without.

He took a few additional steps and re-opened his eyes figuring the doorway was now behind him. For a moment, he feared one of the creatures might be looking around the doorway at him and he imagined its long slimy fingers reaching for the back of his neck. Immediately he repeated the phrase in his mind, "There's nothing to be afraid of. God's always with me." He imagined the thing pulling its fingers back as if it had just touched a scalding hot stove. It was working! Tommy's new weapon from Sunday school was fighting back the evil creatures.

With a newfound confidence, he continued to walk down the hall repeating his mantra and feeling an invisible shield forming around him like a giant glowing shell of protection. When he was about four feet from his bedroom doorway, he considered running the remaining distance past the bathroom and into the safety of his bedroom. He had done that many times in the past. But suddenly he changed his mind. He now believed he was protected and knew the Lurkers couldn't touch him. He wanted to beat back this fear once and for all and decided if he could look his fears directly in the face he could destroy them.

He stopped in front of his bedroom doorway knowing the bathroom was now directly to his left. He thought he could hear the Lurkers inside in the dark, their squirrel like chittering sounds echoing in his mind. It was now or never time to put up or shut up. He repeated his phrase trying to block out the sounds of the creatures, "There's nothing to be afraid of. God's always with me. There's nothing to be afraid of. God's always with me."

Tommy pivoted on his heels and looked directly into the darkness of the bathroom staring hard and daring of the horrid beings to come forward and challenge him and his power. But there was nothing; nothing but the darkness of the empty bathroom. He had done it. He had made it all the way down the hall without any incident and now most, if not all of his fear was gone. He had beaten the hall, he had beaten the Lurkers and they would never be able to frighten him again.

He started to turn with confidence to go to his room when he heard someone call his name. The voice sounded old and raspy and barely human.

"Tommy" the harsh voice chittered.

He was unable to complete his turn frozen in fear at the sound coming from the darkness. He tried to recall his mantra tried to repeat his mystical phrase but couldn't. He imagined his protective shell splitting with millions of tiny cracks and falling apart piece by piece.

Again, he heard his name, "Tommy." He had never before heard it said in such a terrible way.

As he stood frozen staring into the darkness he saw the fingers, the long waving slimy fingers snaking their way toward him out of the blackness. Again he tried to recall his mantra but couldn't; his mind had gone completely blank. Behind the creeping hands, Tommy saw blood red eyes glowing in the darkness. The dancing fingers came out of the doorway into the hall and each hand reached out and touched the sides of Tommy's face as his mother had lovingly done many times in the past. But there was nothing loving about this ice cold and clammy touch. He felt the fingers were sucking the heat from Tommy's body as he began to tremble; the red eyes coming ever closer.

Now the dead hands supported Tommy's convulsing body as his legs gave out under him. The last thing Tommy remembered seeing was an enormous mouth full of hundreds of needle-like teeth opening wide and coming toward his face and a foul sulfur-like odor coming from deep inside the thing. Then his vision went completely black.

"Tommy, here's your lunch," his mother said in her most cheerful voice. She sat on the edge of his bed next to Tommy as she had done every day for the past several months. Tommy didn't answer; he never did. He simply sat staring out into the hall his once brown hair now a shock of pure white; his once intelligent face now appearing slack-jawed and catatonic. Soft mushy food dribbled down his chin with a stream of drool. On occasion, his lips would move and seemed to be repeating some type of phrase but his parents were unable to make out what he said.

WHENCE COMETH THE WOLF?

Morning brought a new day complete with the bright sun rising over the eastern hillside casting its warm glow across the acres of cornfield as the cool moist evening dew clung desperately to the tall blades of grass along the sloping ridge. Birds chirped their good morning songs while in the distance you could hear the sounds of people waking to greet another day from the nearby housing subdivision.

In the tall grass atop the hill, a man rustled groggily awakening from his night's sleep. One eye fluttered open, and he saw the sunlit morning through long bunches of weedy grass growing wild around his face. On the side of one particular long weed, a young grasshopper clung seeming to stare curiously at the man.

A chill ran through his body, and he became aware he was lying in the wet dewy grass completely naked. Remaining perfectly still not daring to get up from his prone position, Lonnie Talbert tried to analyze the situation and determine where he might be and just how bad things were this time.

As he lay quietly, he heard the cawing of several birds, and listening more intently, he could hear the buzzing of insects perhaps bees, no it seemed to be flies; hundreds of them. His stomach lurched with realization of the implications of what he was hearing. Slowly he lifted his head ever so slightly and over the tops of the tall weeds, he could see several large black birds perhaps ten of them all busy picking and pulling at something in the grass a few feet away. His heart skipped a beat at the comprehension of what had likely happened yet again as it had happened for the first time a month ago.

Rising up on two hands supporting himself with his arms, he looked uncertainly across the top of the tall grass and saw what he feared most. Two of the black birds were fighting over a long stringy morsel of pinkish gray food. They each had their beaks clamped on a piece of intestine and were having a ghastly tug-of-war with it.

Within one second, Lonnie saw the complete picture. On a blanket not five feet from him, lay the body of a naked woman her stomach ripped open; her entrails spilled onto the blanket, blood splattered everywhere. Her body was a brutal landscape of gashes and rips leaving her scarcely recognizable as human.

Her mouth hung agape, her dark blue tongue hanging loosely from an opening enlarged by a long deep red gouge leading down to her neck where muscle hung loosely like strands of thick spaghetti. Flies swarmed around her face and several could be seen crawling along her lolling tongue. One of her eyes stared sightlessly upward through a film of death while the other dangled by thin bloody filaments down along the side of her cheek. One of the black birds had perched on her forehead and started pecking at the filaments with the hopes of snagging the soft juicy prize.

Large clumps of the woman's hair with pieces of scalp still attached lay strewn about the blanket her skull nothing more than a revolting patchwork of blood-covered white spaces where the scalp had once resided. Scores of blue and green flies walked freely along the bloody areas drinking, laying eggs and doing whatever else the vile insects did in such a situation.

Her right arm lay stretched back alongside her battered head, the left arm was ripped off at the shoulder and lay in the grass perhaps ten or twenty feet away from the body. Another cluster of birds was pecking and feasting on it off in the distance. From the torn flesh of the place where the arm was formerly located, white bone jutted obtrusively.

Above the mangled abdominal area was a flat patch of blood and muscles where her breasts should have been. Lonnie didn't even want to venture a guess what might have happened to them. Oddly, her legs remained intact and strangely still quite beautiful. The contrast between her legs and the horrifically bloody remains was startling.

"What was her name?" he thought to himself unable to recall.

Lonnie looked down at his own body and saw blood covered him; what seemed like gallons of gore.

"Not again!" Lonnie cried. "Not again! Why does this keep happening to me?"

Staying as low to the ground as possible he searched through the tall grass for his clothing and found them on a pile mixed up with the girl's all damp from the cool evening but at least still intact. He took the girl's white printed dress and with the wetness still lingering on the grass washed as much of the blood off his body as possible then tossed the garment aside. Still incredibly chilled from the cold, he put on his damp clothing and ran stooped over toward the nearby road where he saw a car parked.

He recalled it was the girl's car. "Thank goodness." Lonnie thought. He was lucky no one had driven by and checked on the car or had seen him lying there naked as the day he was born covered in blood. He climbed into the car seeing she had left the keys in the ignition. He started the engine and turned on the heater. Cold air came flooding from the vents chilling him further. He turned down the fan giving the heater a chance to warm up. Looking back toward the place where the body lay he was satisfied to see from the road nothing looked out of the ordinary the body well hidden in the tall grass. It might be a number of days or weeks until someone actually discovered her, and by then he would be long gone, again.

As he drove away, he tried to remember the events of the previous evening before he had blacked out. He recalled his cousin Ron dropping him off at a local bar on his way to work. Ron worked third shift at a local factory. His cousin's schedule actually worked out well for Lonnie since he was a night owl by nature. Lonnie said he'd take a cab home. He'd met the girl (What was her name, Sarah? Sally? Sandy?), and they had hit it off immediately. Then after a few drinks and a little slow dancing, they headed out to her car.

She had brought him out to the rural hilltop site pulled over and had taken a thick blanket from the trunk. Walking down into the tall grass overlooking the cornfield,

they had lain down on the blanket and gotten to know
each other much better. The last thing he recalled was
lying on his back in the grass afterward and looking up at
the beautiful full moon. Then he must have blacked out
just like had happened the previous month. That led him
to think about the events of the previous month.

Although that had been a completely different situation,
the results were no less horrific. He remembered how he
had been walking home to his apartment after another late
night at a local New York City bar. He had been laid off
from his job several months earlier and didn't really have a
set schedule or any reason to get up in the morning so he
tended to stay out late and then slept most of the day.

As he turned a corner to take a short cut down an alley,
several thugs dressed in gang colors stopped him
encircling him. Once they had surrounded him, each of
them brandishing knifes they told him to give them his
wallet or they would cut him, and cut him good. He saw
their deadly blades gleaming in the light of the full moon.
Then the first blackout came.

When he awoke the next morning he was in the same
alley with his clothing shredded soaked in blood and with
barely enough material remaining to keep the clothes on
his body. At first based on the condition of his clothing, he
thought perhaps the gang had actually cut him and
somehow he had survived. Yet he felt no pain and none of
the blood appeared to be his. Standing and looking around
as the sun slowly climbed in the sky its beams entering the
alley from between the tall city buildings; he saw the
carnage laid out before him.

The alley looked as though it had been the scene of a
jet airliner crash. Severed limbs and body parts were
scattered around the blood-soaked street. Lonnie saw
several headless torsos with their slick entrails piled next
to them. Not four feet from where he stood the head of the
gang member who had threatened him stared lifelessly at
him through gray-filmed eyes. Sewer rats the size of small
cats wandered from body to body, sampling bits of flesh
and innards. Some were eating the eyes from other severed
heads. Lonnie turned his head bent and vomited onto the
street. He looked at the regurgitated mess and saw it was

blood red in color. Upon closer inspection, he thought he saw a piece of a human ear floating among the filth.

He staggered down the alley making it back to his apartment just a few blocks away without being seen. Once there he showered and disposed of the bloody rags that were once his clothing then took another long hot shower. Afterwards he realized just how exhausted he was and collapsed in bed where he fell fast asleep. Horrible images he couldn't begin to explain riddled his dreams. He saw the gang members screaming and being torn to pieces; seeing all of this as if through his own eyes. Throughout the scattered flashing images, he heard growling of a wild animal. He woke up later that morning hearing police sirens approaching. Staggering to the window, he saw a number of patrol cars converging on the alley several blocks away. He knew what they had found.

The only thing he could think to do was to get out of the city for a while. He got dressed and packed a duffle bag with essentials. He had no idea what had happened or why he had blacked out, but after seeing what he had vomited, he knew somehow the carnage he saw was of his own making.

He called his cousin Ron in Pennsylvania and asked if he could come to visit for a few weeks. Ron lived in an apartment in a few miles west of the city of Reading. Ron knew Lonnie was a night owl and they would both be sleeping during the day, which wouldn't cause any interruption of his third-shift lifestyle. So he agreed for Lonnie to visit for a short while.

Lonnie caught the next Amtrak train to Philadelphia then he took a bus to Reading and finally took a cab to Ron's apartment. After the first two weeks, Ron agreed Lonnie could stay for a few extra weeks longer since things had been going so smoothly. That was until the previous evening.

Now Lonnie was back where he started a month earlier confused, frustrated and suffering with guilt over yet another death; and this time it wasn't a group of thugs bent on hurting him but a defenseless woman. He drove away in the dead girl's car from the latest unspeakable scene and contemplated what he should do next. He had to figure out what was wrong with him, and there was definitely something very wrong. Up until two months earlier, his life had been typical and normal; that was obviously no longer the case. Because if he truly was responsible for the savagery he had witnessed at each of those horrible events, Lonnie would have to do something.

He turned up the fan on the car heater enjoying the warm air surrounding him taking away the chill and helping to dry his clothing. When he got to Ron's apartment, he crept inside being careful not to wake him and gathered up all of his belongings. Then he wrote a note thanking Ron but saying he needed to get back to the city, start looking for another job and get his life back on track.

Then Lonnie took his meager belongings and climbed back into the girl's car pointing it in the direction of New York City. As he drove, he thought more about when all the strangeness had started trying to pinpoint an incident, which might have served as a catalyst to trigger the horrid events. The only weird thing he could recall was the incident, which happened three months earlier with that weird Goth chick at the nightclub.

Lonnie had stopped by one of the city's slightly freaky nightclubs after hearing a number of his buddies bragging about the quality of the girls frequenting the place. He hadn't been disappointed. The place was crawling with some of the hottest women he had seen in a long time. Lonnie was standing by the bar waiting for his drink when an incredibly attractive Goth-looking girl approached him and without preamble kissed him smack on the lips prying his lips open with her tongue then sending said tongue halfway down his throat.

He stood looking at her in shock for a moment then introduced himself and offered to buy her a drink learning her name was Cassandra. Next thing he knew they were in an alley behind the bar up and he had her pressed against a brick wall. He recalled she was like a wild animal and things were going great until she bit him hard on the shoulder. Not a love bite or anything of that nature but a full on sink your teeth in and draw blood type of bite.

That act alone, put a damper on what might have proven to be a pleasant event. Lonnie had pushed her away fighting back the urge to haul off and punch her in the face. However, his mother had raised him never to hit a woman, even a psycho bitch like that one. He recalled she had backed down the alley laughing at him.

As she walked away she said something like, "I'll be seeing you again, Lonnie. I chose you. You're one of us now."

He had no idea what she meant by the remark and at the time passed it off as a wacky comment from a crazy chick.

Now, driving up I-95 toward New York, Lonnie started to wonder what she had meant. He certainly had changed since that event.

"I chose you. You're one of us now." he heard the strange girl say in his mind again.

He looked over at the passenger's seat and for a second he saw the Goth chick sitting there smiling at him with blood running down her chin and her eyes glowing yellow-red like a wild animal's. For a moment, he almost lost control of the car but managed to regain his composure. Then the girl was gone. The last thing he needed was to be pulled over by a cop in a dead girl's car.

Speaking of the car, Lonnie had formulated a plan to take the car to any one of several choice neighborhoods in the city. He was going to wipe off all of his fingerprints and then leave it there with the windows open and the keys in the ignition. He then planned to take the subway back to his hotel. He figured it might take all of a half hour for the thing to disappear never to be seen again

Lonnie arrived back in the Big Apple shortly after noon. Then after dumping the car, he returned home walking up the stairs to his apartment exhausted. As he entered the apartment, he noticed something strange. He couldn't explain it, but the hair seemed to rise on the back of his neck and his senses tingled; he somehow knew he wasn't alone. He walked into his living room and found the Goth chick Cassandra from three months earlier relaxing in his favorite chair.

"Hi, Lonnie," she said with a comfortable attitude suggesting they were old friends and her being in his apartment was normal.

"What are you doing here?" he asked, still a bit shocked to see her.

"Why, silly, I've been waiting for you to come home." She slowly rose from the chair and walked toward him. She ran her fingers along the buttons of his shirt sensually. "I was starting to think you might never come back to me."

Lonnie pushed her hands down and said sternly, "Look Cassandra. I don't know what you think you're doing here but this isn't your home and you've got no business being here."

"Oh, Lonnie," she said with a smile, "you just don't seem to understand. I like you. I mean I really like you a lot. That's why I chose you, and why we'll be together from now on."

Lonnie thought aloud, "That's what you said the night we met. You said you'd chosen me. What did it mean? What are you talking about?"

Cassandra asked with a quizzical expression, "Tell me, Lonnie. Has anything strange happened to you lately you can't seem to explain? Maybe something you did or think you might have done, which might be considered out of character for you."

Lonnie saw the dead gang members and the dead girl flash across his mind. Then he saw Cassandra looking at him with recognition as if she could read his thoughts.

She said coyly, "Oh my, Lonnie. Have you been a bad boy? Did you maybe have a nasty run in a month or so ago with some bad gang members?"

"How did you know about . . ." Lonnie stopped himself before saying more than he wanted to.

Cassandra continued, "How did I know about that, you wanted to ask? Well I knew about it because I was there. Yes, I was right there with you."

"Y . . . y . . . you . . . w . . . w . . . were . . . th . . . th . . . there?" he stammered.

"Yes, sir-ee! I was right there by your side," she informed him, "and I planned on being with you last night as well, but for some reason you weren't around. Which means you likely got yourself into some trouble all by our lonesome, I suppose."

Lonnie's head was spinning, "What's going on, Casandra? What's wrong with me? Why is all this happening to me?" He wanted to bolt from the room and leave this strange woman behind, but he had to get to the bottom of this.

"I'd better explain this all to you, Lonnie," she replied. "You see that night at the club in the alley, remember? Well it was time for me to choose a mate, and there was something about you, I found so irresistible I couldn't help myself. So I decided right then and there to choose you to be my mate."

"Choose a mate?" Lonnie said questioning. "You bit me on the shoulder and you, you drew blood."

"Oh, I did a lot more than, Lonnie, my sweet," she said. "Do you know what a lycanthrope is?"

Lonnie thought for a moment then replied, "A lycanthrope? No is it some sort of plant or something?"

Cassandra chuckled, "No, Lonnie. A lycanthrope is a shape shifter, what you know as a werewolf. I'm a werewolf, and now thanks to me you're one too."

"That's ridiculous!" Lonnie argued. "It's all nonsense and old wives' tales. You know, it's nothing but a legend. It isn't real."

"Lonnie. I want you to think real hard about what happened in the alley last month and what probably happened to you last night. Those were both nights of full moons. That's why you changed. You changed so you could hunt. I was there for your first kill in the alley. I was there to help you, although to be honest you really didn't need much help. I just had to take care of one or two of them who almost got away. But you were a natural."

Lonnie stood staring in shock, "But I don't recall much of any of what happened."

"That's typical. But soon you'll become more aware, and then you'll look forward to the change with great anticipation. Eventually when you become more experienced, you'll be able to change at will and won't need the help of the full moon. Then you'll know you've become complete."

Lonnie contemplated, "And I'm supposed to be your mate?"

"Yes. I've marked you so none of the others will try to claim you. "

"Others?" He questioned.

Cassandra explained, "Yes, others. We're a pack. We live together, hunt together and take care of each other. You won't need to worry about your old life any longer: your job, your friends, your family, or this apartment. You'll come to live with the pack, and we'll show you the way of the wolf. We'll teach you to use your new powers. We'll turn you into a great hunter and perhaps someday you might be king of the pack, and when that happens, I'll be your queen."

"But I don't want to hunt and kill people. It's not who I am."

"It may not be who you were," she said, "but it's who you are now. Here let me to prove it to you."

Cassandra walked to the door leading to Lonnie's bedroom. She slowly opened the door, and Lonnie was shocked to see a beautiful young woman tied and gagged spread out naked on his bed her arms and legs bound to the four posts. The bound woman looked at him with fear of anticipation at what was to come. There were cuts at various locations along her body and blood stained the bed sheets.

"Now, Lonnie," Cassandra said, "you need to accept who you are. You need to embrace the wolf within you. You need to hunt. You need to kill."

Lonnie's sense of smell reached a level he never believed possible. He could smell the girl's blood. He could smell her sweat. He could smell her fear. His sight could see beyond her physical presence seeing a type of reddish orange glow surround her obviously brought on by her fear. He could hear her heart thumping hard inside her chest and could feel his own heart begin to thump harder in anticipation.

"That's it, Lonnie," Cassandra prodded. "Smell her blood, Lonnie. Let the fever grow inside you. You want to feast on her flesh, Lonnie. Change, Lonnie, change!" Cassandra's voice grew louder with each shout of encouragement.

Lonnie could feel the change starting. He looked down at his hands and saw his fingers lengthening, darkening in color and becoming leathery in appearance as his nails grew out into long yellowed razor sharp claws. Turning his hands over, he saw coarse animal-hair sprouting from the backs of them. He felt his canine teeth getting longer the bottom ones protruding upward from his salivating lower jaw. He kicked off his shoes to stop the pain he was feeling in his feet as they enlarged in size their nails growing to mirror the claws on his hands. He felt the urge to kill, to rip apart, to savage the helpless girl now tied to his bed. The smell of her blood was driving him into an uncontrollable frenzy.

With the roar of a wild beast he had become, Lonnie jumped up onto the bed eager to begin feasting on the entrails of the powerless victim. He stood over her body looking down into her pleading eyes. Then in an instant the night before came back to him and in his mind's eye he saw what he had done to the woman in Pennsylvania and was sickened by what he recalled. He understood this is what he had become. This is what Cassandra had turned him into; a savage grunting slobbering beast bent on slaughtering anyone and anything in his path. Standing over the naked woman, he raised his clawed hand high above his head bringing it down quickly and slicing through the bonds securing her to the bed.

Then in one rapid motion, he turned and lunged at Cassandra slashing and tearing at her with a fury he had never known before. He savagely gouged and cut her as blood and flaps of skin flew in every direction. He noticed she had begun to transform to her wolf form. As she changed, the wounds he had inflicted began to close up and miraculously heal right before his eyes. Lonnie understood, if he didn't act quickly before the transformation was complete she would likely kill him, as she was much more experienced at being a werewolf than he was.

Lonnie did the only thing he could think of. He buried his claws deep into her still human chest shattering her ribs into fragments then he ripped her heart from its cavity brought it to his mouth and devoured it before her dying eyes. Cassandra collapsed to the floor in a heap as the transformation reversed itself and she returned to her human appearance blood pooling on the floor next to her tattered remains.

Lonnie was suddenly aware of the other woman screaming. He turned to see her cowering in the corner in shock with tears streaming down her face. The urge to fall on her and rip her to shreds was almost more than Lonnie could suppress, but he was determined to keep hold of this remaining bit of his humanity. He began slowly transforming back to his human self as he gathered shoes and clothing and raced from the apartment.

Lonnie understood the life he once enjoyed was over forever. When the police found Cassandra's body in his apartment the authorities would be after him. When the "pack" of werewolves found out what he had done to Cassandra, they too would likely try to hunt him down. He'd have to get out of town and away from any friends relatives or ties to his previous life. He'd be on the run, "a lone wolf," he thought to himself with a self-deprecating laugh. He had no idea, what his life would be like from then on, but he was determined to find a way to keep the wolf inside him at bay and never hurt another human again. He could only hope he would be successful.

THE DEMON OF COOGAN'S MINE

Night had fallen bringing darkness with the intensity to make even the most resolute of men wonder if perhaps nature itself was offering an omen of impending doom. Coldness hung in the air on the late October 1961 evening sending chills down the spine of the lone man standing in silhouette beneath the dim glow of a security light hanging high on the nearby utility pole.

The man had walked up the winding access road following it toward a plateau, which intersected with a rising hillside where a timber-framed doorway stood, once the entrance to a coalmine long since abandoned. He stared at the rusted rails extending out from the opening toward him beckoning him to come inside. This was all that remained of the once prosperous Coogan Coal Mine, which thrived in the later part of the nineteenth century until one of the area's worst mine disasters resulted in its closing in 1885.

On a rotting timber, crowning the entrance hung a painted sign, worn and barely legible reading, "Co ___ n's Mine." A bloody handprint obscured the missing letters. Several similar red painted handprints stippled the two mine doors, which dangled wretchedly askew.

Mounted on one wooden door was a washed out sign warning "UNSAFE MINE - KEEP OUT." Graffiti covered the doors as well spouting admonitions such as "Doorway to Hell," "Devil Dan's Hell Hole," "Soul Sucker," "Death Awaits You" and "Turn Back Now." Layers of coal dust and spider webs coated the access as insects crawled in and out of the decomposing wood.

Sam stood stock-still, apprehensive. He had grown up hearing all the stories about the mine about its history and its legend. Everyone in Ashton, not to mention all of Schuylkill County Pennsylvania, had heard about the legend of Coogan's mine. He wasn't one to believe in folklore and such superstitious nonsense, yet having heard the stories repeatedly since childhood, Sam felt uneasy especially on such a dark and foreboding night.

Sam Hughes was what most local people would describe as a "shiftless" sort of character. At the age of twenty-five, he had never held a "real" job, so to speak. He was one of those people who seemed somehow to survive quite nicely, without any known means of income. Some townspeople suspected he might have been "on relief" as was the local term for someone on welfare but this wasn't the case.

Some thought perhaps Sam was involved with some element of crime either robbery, drugs, whatever, and as a result, he was always under the watchful eye of Ashton Chief of Police, Max Seiler who also believed perhaps everything wasn't quite on the up and up with the strange young man.

Sam often laughed to himself about all the talk about him from the townspeople. "If they only knew," he often thought to himself. If they knew the truth, they would likely shun him and treat him with even less respect if that was possible. But at least they might stop spreading their malicious stories, but then again what fun would that be?

The real secret to Sam's ability to live his life without working was simple. His mother Suzanne had been a housekeeper at one time for one of the wealthiest families in the county, the Coogan family. Bill Coogan, grandson of Irish immigrant Big Bill Coogan, the original owner of the mine was very wealthy having grown the family business substantially since his father's death. He now ran the business under the name Coogan Oil and Petroleum. Coogan also owned most of the prime land in the county not to mention most of the local police as well as many of the county judges.

Bill Coogan had been a rowdy young man in his youth and had made the mistake of impregnating Suzanne. Her parents had approached old man Coogan threatening to make trouble if he didn't offer some form of restitution. The old man had paid them off by buying them a nice house. He also provided a substantial monthly stipend to help them raise the baby. The conditions of the agreement were the monthly payment would continue all of the child's life even into adulthood as long as they promised to keep the secret of the baby's paternity and not come looking for any additional money than the agreed amount. Old man Coogan's lawyer had been present to make sure the deal was legal and binding.

After Suzanne's parents passed away, she stayed in the house raising then teenage Sam on her own, and after she died of cancer when Sam was twenty, he continued to live in the house and enjoy the monthly allotments as well. Once after Suzanne's death Bill Coogan had tried to stop the payments, but Sam was quick to confront the man making sure his mysterious income would continue especially since Bill now had a wife and family to think about. After all God only knew what an angry Mrs. Coogan might do to poor Bill if the truth came out.

He didn't mind taking the money either as in Sam's opinion it was his birthright to be Bill Coogan IV, a title which now fell on Coogan's young nine-year-old son, Billy, Sam's half-brother. Sam realized this boy would inherit a virtual empire someday, so why should he feel bad about getting a small portion of what was rightfully his?

Sam stood staring at the entrance to the mine contemplating what to do next. That damned legend still hung in his mind. Surely, it was complete nonsense, but somehow he was still concerned.

The legend of Coogan's mine dated back to the disaster of 1885 in which twenty-three men lost their lives. Twenty of them died immediately and three more that were trapped in an air chamber formed at the bottom of the mine died before they could be rescued. They recovered two of the three bodies in a mummified state with their stomach cavities ripped apart and empty. The third body was never found; a man called Dan O'Boyle.

Legend had it the missing miner O'Boyle had cursed Big Bill Coogan with his dying breath swearing he would sell his soul to the devil for a chance to get revenge on the Coogan clan. He had apparently done just that, and according to the story, the miner had been transformed into a hulking immortal soul-sucking demon the better to serve his dark master by collecting the souls of the living. The legend said O'Boyle had feasted on the entrails of the last two survivors as part of some demonic ritual.

Unfortunately for O'Boyle, the great deceiver had played a trick on him forcing him to remain in the mine until he was able to gather ninety-nine more souls and gain his freedom. Until that time, if the monster tried to leave the mine, his flesh would be burned from his body causing excruciating and lasting pain for the beast. It appeared Satan wanted the beast to have a long time to learn how to use its various powers before walking out among humans.

According to the local legend, somewhere in the bottom of the mine, which collapsed completely in 1885, dwelled a savage demon waiting to collect his next soul getting him ever closer to his freedom and his chance to have his final vengeance on the Coogan family. Anytime anyone went missing locally, people would look at each other with an unspoken knowing wondering if they might have gone into the mine.

A chill again ran down Sam's spine as he thought to himself, he was in fact a Coogan descendent. If the creature were real, he suspected it would likely recognize him as a Coogan. Sam realized it probably didn't really matter either way since if such a creature actually existed it would make short work of him no matter what his lineage.

Then he chastised himself for following such a ridiculous and unproductive train of thought. There was no demon in this mine; it was all a great lie concocted by locals many years ago and encouraged he suspected by his illegitimate father Bill Coogan Jr. to hide something most likely something of great value deep down inside.

Sam had thought about it long and hard for many months. He knew Coogan was no stranger to doing things that might be just slightly on the wrong side of the law. It was likely he had some cash or other valuables, which he had to keep hidden from the government. Where could he find a better place to hide his treasures than down in the mine? By allowing the story of the demon to spread, he could keep everyone away from the mine and allow his treasure to remain a secret.

He chuckled at the bloody handprints on the door as well as the references to the demon of the mine. Sam wouldn't have been surprised at all to learn Coogan himself had placed those marking on the rotted doors.

But Sam was also no fool being cut from the same cloth as Bill Coogan. He knew the mine was likely still unsafe, and it was very possible some wild animals such as rats and wild cats or perhaps even bears might make their home in that mine so he came prepared. He reached down and opened a sack he had brought with him removing a long flashlight with fresh batteries and a 38-caliber revolver, which his grandfather had given to him when he was twelve years old.

He grandfather had told him, "Sammy. When I ain't here you have to be the man of the house. That means you have to protect your momma and your grandma. This gun will do that for you. If someone breaks in, you shoot him. Don't stop to think about it, just do it. If he tries to get away, then shoot him on the front porch, drag his carcass inside and tell Chief Seiler he was in the house. That should cover you pretty well." His grandfather had taught the young Sam how to shoot, and since the old man's death, he had been practicing regularly with the gun and had become quite proficient.

So Sam stood with his flashlight in his left hand and his revolver in his right. He believed he was ready for anything. He thought about what he might find when he went inside the mine as he cautiously made his way toward the opening. He knew the mine was still likely unsafe but suspected if Coogan really did have some sort of treasure in there he'd have at least shored up that part of the mine so it would provide safe passage.

Sam slowly reached out to open the left mine door which creaked ominously on its rusted hinges, producing a shower of dust and spider webs which he batted out of his way. For a moment, he hesitated and thought if Coogan actually had been in the mine recently then why was there so much dust and why were there so many spider webs? Perhaps Coogan didn't come to the mine that often; maybe only once or twice a year to check on his ill-gotten gains. He supposed that would explain it. In addition, Sam knew spiders could spin their webs very quickly so it might have only been a few weeks since Coogan's last visit.

Using the flashlight, he kept the rotted door propped open so he could fit through keeping his gun at the ready. Suddenly he felt something brush past his right foot and looked down in time to see a huge rat over a foot long scurrying over his shoe. His first instinct was to shoot it, but luckily, he stopped himself just short of accidentally blowing off his own foot.

Being more cautious and alert for any other such surprises Sam entered the mine pulling the door closed behind him. The inside of the mine was nothing like what Sam had expected. Instead of debris and timbers strewn about, the area was completely clear. Shining his flashlight up along the wall toward the ceiling Sam was astonished to see an enormous cylindrical tunnel over twenty feet in diameter had been carved from a vein of coal, sloping downward into the belly of the mine below for a distance far beyond the reach of his flashlight beam.

Sam thought for a few moments about what this might mean and realized not only was the legend a total lie, but Bill Coogan had somehow been actually working this mine for many years and sneaking out the coal while locals assumed the mine was still abandoned. He must have had many men to help him do a job of this magnitude. Sam couldn't figure out how Coogan was doing the mining without anyone in town knowing about it and couldn't imagine any local workers keeping such a secret, but he intended to find out tonight. He assumed somewhere deep down in the mine there must be a second shaft Coogan used to get into this main tunnel.

And what an odd tunnel it was, Sam thought. Instead of a typical timber reinforced mineshaft, this tunnel appeared formed from solid coal and needed no external support to keep its shape. Sam lived in the coal region his entire life and grew up around mining. And although he had no practical work experience in mining and was far from an expert, he had never heard of anything even coming close to this.

Sam continued to work his way down the huge tunnel his gun still in hand though he knew he would only use it if absolutely necessary as surely firing a gun in the sloped chamber of solid coal would be a ricocheting nightmare. When he reached the bottom of the tunnel where it stopped against a solid wall of coal, he noticed it took a ninety-degree right turn.

Using his flashlight as a guide, he walked along the odd continuation of the tunnel, which now seemed no longer to be heading downward but continued horizontally. Up ahead he noticed the tunnel seemed to end at some sort of enormous cave. He cautiously walked out of the tunnel standing on a precipice overlooking the cavern. He shown his light around the cave and was amazed at its incredible size.

Then his light reflected off something and Sam was shocked to see mountains of cracked coal, literally tons of the stuff piled high all around the cave. There had to be several million dollars' worth of coal just waiting to be hauled out of the mine.

"So," he thought to himself, "this is the treasure Coogan was hiding." Black diamonds, as locals called them, tons and tons of coal, already cracked and ready for market.

Sam decided as soon as he found the alternate way out of the mine he was going to put together a plan whereby he and several of his drinking buddies could bootleg this coal and make a fortune, especially since all the work had been done for him.

Suddenly Sam heard a deep sorrowful moaning coming from across the cavern to the right. He shown his light in that direction and was shocked by what he saw. The surface of the far side of the cave seemed to be transforming into some sort of liquid like substance giving off an eerie red glow.

The wall literally began to move as it if were alive. From within the wall fingertips stretched and pushed out toward him then retreated inward again. Then Sam saw a smooth and stretched image of a man's face begin to protrude from the wall wearing an expression of unbearable sorrow. Then it too quickly sucked back into the wall once again.

Then more hands and fingers appeared and disappeared. The entire wall burst into a mass of writhing faces, arms, legs and other body parts all seeming to come and go bubbling up from some sort of Hell-spawned ooze. This was occurring impossibly along a vertical wall somehow defying gravity. These apparent tortured creatures stretched as far as they possibly could in a feeble attempt to escape but were instantly pulled back into the pulsing wall. None of the creatures appeared to have a single hair anywhere on their bodies. Although naked, the beings were without visible sex organs permitting no way to distinguish between male and female. All of these horrible creatures seemed to be performing a hideous ballet of sorrow just under the red liquid skin-like surface of the wall.

Sam watched the spectacle in horror realizing he was looking at the "Wall Of Lost Souls" he had heard described in the local legend of Coogan's mine. If that part of the story were true, then he understood the part about the demon of the mine was true as well. It was time for him to get out of Dodge. Sam turned to head back the way he came. Coal or no coal, treasure or no treasure, he had to get out of the mine and get out immediately.

As he turned to go down the tunnel, he heard a grunting noise and deep animal-like breathing coming directly from the blackness of the tunnel in front of him. He smelled a musky odor, deep and feral combined with what smelled like rotten meat. He raised his flashlight and shown it around inside the huge tunnel, not seeing anything until he suddenly caught a reflection high near the top of the tunnel like the glow of an animal's eyes in headlights.

An incredible ear-splitting roar bellowed from deep in the tunnel, and Sam heard the tremendous pounding of footfalls, like those of a massive beast heading right toward him. He raised his gun to shoot but before he could do so, an enormous human-like hand with six-inch long claws seized his arm snapping it at the wrist. His gun rattled to the floor, and Sam screamed in pain as another clawed hand wrapped around Sam's throat not in a strangling grip but one meant only to subdue him. He had little doubt if this creature wanted him dead, he would have been dead already, and knowing what he did about the legend, he understood with great regret, he would have been much better off if the creature had killed him outright.

Sam's flashlight dropped to the floor of the cave providing just enough light for Sam to see his terrible attacker. The thing was repulsive beyond comprehension. Sam had never seen or even dreamt of such a beast in his worst nightmares. The creature had a pushed up snout like a pig with large flaring nostrils, which seemed to open and close with each foul breath it took. The demon had yellow-red eyes sunken in dark holes and long pointed black ears curling back away from its face. On top of its head was a massive mane of long black hair flowing matted down its back. Covering its face was a tangled beard caked with crud and crawling with insects and maggots.

There were two curved horns protruding from either side of his forehead near the top of its skull ram-like in appearance. The creature's huge mouth was full of long fanged teeth the bottom row having two huge tusks protruding upward over its top lip.

The creature stared into Sam's eyes for just a moment then slowly tilted its head, turning it to the side flaring its nostrils as it sniffed the air.

"Coogan!" The thing said in a low guttural voice, "You are a Coogan! I can smell it on you."

Sam was paralyzed with fear and unable to utter a single word. The creature threw him hard to the floor of the cave where his right leg snapped upon impact causing Sam intolerable pain. Sam screamed, and the creature stood looking down at him its shape still visible in the fallen flashlight. The beast was a massive thing almost twenty feet tall standing naked hovering over him its leather-like skin glistening with sweat. Its arms were long, and they practically hung to the ground where Sam saw its huge feet also armed with similar talon-like claws. He realized it must have been the demon who had dug out the tunnels. He didn't understand how or why the thing had kept the coal, but he no longer cared as his agony was too great.

Finally, Sam tried to speak through his pain in order to beg for his life. "Please don't kill me," he cried. "I'm not really a Coogan. I hate Bill Coogan as much as you do. I know who you are. You're Dan O'Boyle. You were once as human as I am."

The creature looked at him curiously and said in a deep throaty rasp, "Dan O'Boyle? That's a name I have not heard for a long time. Dan O'Boyle is dead. He died in this mine back in 1885. I may have once been Dan, but now I am so much more than Dan could ever be. Dan O'Boyle is dead"

Sam noticed his gun on the ground reflecting in the light from his fallen flashlight and decided to try and keep the creature busy long enough for him to squirm closer and perhaps grab the weapon. His shattered leg and wrist ached with incredible pain, but he had to find a way.

"But I hate the Coogans, I tell you," Sam repeated. "I'm the illegitimate son of Bill Coogan. He doesn't even acknowledge me. I'm like you. If I had the chance, I'd kill Bill Coogan with my own bare hands."

The creature looked surprised and said, "Are you telling me you're Bill Coogan's bastard son?" Then the demon seemed to be contemplating this for a moment distracted. "Maybe there is some way I can use you to get what I want from Bill Coogan."

"Please just let me live," Sam pleaded, "and I'll do whatever you want. I swear I will." Sam saw the gun was now within his reach.

The creature bent lower to get a closer look at Sam when he made his move and grabbed for the gun with his still working left hand. In one practiced motion brought it around and shot the creature directly in the throat. The thunderous sound made by the revolver in the cavern was deafening.

The creature fell to his knees on the ground in front of Sam grabbing Sam's gun hand engulfing it but not hurting him. The creature stared down directly into the man's eyes without moving or showing any sign of life. Sam looked on in disbelief. The demon appeared to be in a trance.

Sam saw the huge three-inch hole the shot made in the creature's throat. Smoke poured from the fissure and the surrounding flesh was smoldering from the blast. Then Sam saw the hole begin to change. First, he heard the buzzing of insects as maggots began to crawl from the opening dropping one by one to the floor of the cave. Then greenish-blue colored flies, the kind Sam had seen in the past feasting on road kill began to emerge from the wound and swarmed around the creature's throat.

Then just as quickly the swarm funneled back into the gaping wound. Then the flies started linking themselves together forming a type of netting over the opening closing it as the beast's flesh began to crawl from the edges of the hole across the web of flies to the center completely closing the opening.

Once again the beast regained its focus as a sinister smile appeared on its leathery lips, "Oh, you poor sad bastard of a Coogan. You think something as trivial as a gun can kill me? I am immortal. I am forever."

With that, the creature tore the gun from Sam's left hand ripping out several of the man's fingers at the same time. Blood poured from the places where the fingers once were and white bones jutted from the stumps. Sam screamed in agony.

The creature lifted Sam by the throat holding him suspended about ten feet off the ground, Sam's mangled leg and shattered arms dangling uselessly. He stared directly into the demon's yellow and red eyes the legend coming back to him in its entirety, as he understood what was going to happen to him next. It was the ritual; the ceremony the creature had to perform in order to steal Sam's life force, his very soul. He also understood his soul would go into the horrid wall across the cavern to be stored with the rest of the lost souls until the demon's dark master came to collect them.

The creature held Sam in front of his horrible face. Sam's stomach turned at the foul odor emanating from the demon a combination of decomposing flesh, sulfur and death. Sam could feel the creature's claws climbing slowly up his side stopping at his stomach area. With a quick swipe, the beast sliced through Sam's shirt and flesh making four large gashes in his abdomen. Blood flowed freely from the gashes, and Sam could feel the warm wetness running down his legs.

He wanted to scream from the incredible pain but was unable to because of the creature had a vice-like grip on his throat. A moment later, Sam felt his intestines let go as his entrails tumbled from his body and were caught by the waiting hand of the demon, who played with them, letting them slide through his fingers.

Sam felt weakness setting in, as he knew his life was ending. The creature came closer to him opening his ghastly foul mouth wide in anticipation. Sam saw several glowing white sparkles leaving his own mouth traveling across the air and into the mouth of the creature. Then the sparkles became more abundant eventually becoming a steady stream of white light. Soon the stream began to diminish and the last living thought Sam had was, "The legend is true. The demon of Coogan's mine is real."

Suddenly Sam awoke finding himself in a place of blood red color and chaos. All around him were many unrecognizable beings floating in a gelatinous reddish liquid bumping into one another, some moaning, some crying and some screaming in extreme grief.

He pushed his way past several of the beings each one screaming or moaning incessantly. He saw light off to his left and swam through the gelatinous goo in that direction. He pressed his fingers against a thin membrane stretching it out as far as he could, but it wouldn't give way. He needed to see what was happening so he pressed his face against the film straining to see outside. He saw something far off in the distance.

It was his flashlight far away apparently across the great cavern. Next to it, he saw the creature kneeling over his dead body feasting on his disemboweled entrails. His body no longer looked as it once had but appeared shriveled and mummified. As the creature finished its feast, it looked up seeing Sam in the Wall Of Lost Souls and let out an ear-piercing howl. Sam soon found himself moaning and crying mournfully, joining the chorus of lost souls trapped helplessly for eternity in the wall.

HAPPY VALENTINE'S DAY

The sun was a burning ball of orange fire as it set slowly in the western sky. Its fiery light pierced through the small spaces between weathered planks of lumber nailed securely across the window frames. The setting sunlight was the only thing capable of finding its way inside the sheltered building.

Across the room from the window, a young man in his late twenties sat quietly in a large wooden rocking chair with a sawed-off shotgun lying across his lap at the ready. The slow rhythmic rocking of the chair had a soothing effect because of its continuous back and forth motion. The man sat staring at light filtering into the darkening room. The rocker moved back and forth, back and forth, back and forth.

The man, Roger Washburn shook his head to break the chair's hypnotic spell and cautiously got to his feet listening, turning his head from side to side. He slowly set the shotgun down across the arms of the rocker and approached the boarded window still listening, ever vigilant. With some trepidation, he peeked through one of the cracks between the boards to try to get a better view of the beautiful sunset. There was very little beauty in the world anymore, so Roger tried to make a point to enjoy the simple things the world still had to offer whenever possible such as a beautiful sunset, especially since he never knew when it might be the last one he might ever see.

Looking through one of the small cracks Roger saw the sun in the distance its stunning glow a sharp contrast to the horrible destruction permeating the once beautiful cityscape illuminated under its light. The city was in ruins, a charred and ravaged shell of the great metropolis it had once been. As he had done a thousand times before and would probably do a thousand times again, Roger wondered how so much destruction could have happened so quickly. He rested his head and his hand against the wooden planking releasing a cheerless, frustrated sigh.

Wham! A hand slammed savagely against the outside of the planking rattling the boards against Rogers' head causing him to jump back in surprise. Pain shot through the front of his skull where the board had wobbled and struck him.

"Jesus!" Roger shouted.

Though he was startled, he was much more than that; he was angry with himself for letting his guard down. He knew better. Perhaps it was the human need for things to be back to normal. Whatever the cause, he knew he never should have gotten so close to the boarded window since it allowed his scent to escape out into the world out there to "them" to where "they" now ruled. They could smell his humanity. They could smell his living flesh, and that smell was intoxicating for them.

He stood quietly trying to calm his heavy breathing. He waited for a few minutes to see if the thing outside the window would leave or if it would attempt to break in. He realized how foolish he was to imagine the thing would give up. They never gave up, as they were mindless eating machines.

After a few moments, he heard a familiar groaning sound these beasts all seemed to make and then heard the thing scraping its fleshless bone-exposed fingers along the outside of the boards trying to find a way inside. Scratch, scratch, scratch went the sickening sound of bone against wood.

Roger knew he had to act quickly. For the moment he was fairly sure there was only one of them out there. But he knew if he waited too much longer, others would take notice to the commotion and drag themselves over to see what was happening. Then there would be several all moaning, groaning and scraping their claws against the wood. Some might bang their fists against the planking and some might even figure out how to devise pry bars and try to pull the boards apart. Then before too long there'd be hundreds of them, and if that happened, then it would be all over. The fat lady would have sung as they say, and Roger wasn't ready to hear that tune at least, not just yet anyway.

Reaching down alongside of the window frame Roger grabbed a long thin iron rod about a half-inch in diameter complete with a handgrip he had fashioned himself by bending the rod to fit his grasp perfectly. He had sharpened the business end of the bar to a rapier thin point. He had no idea what the original purpose of rod was in its past life, but he understood what it was used for now since he had altered it for this specific purpose. He positioned the point of the tool in a space between two boards and stood quietly waiting for just the right moment.

Outside the scraping and moaning continued. After a few seconds the scraping stopped, and he saw an eye peering through one of the spaces its lens covered with a grey film of death. Without a moment's hesitation Roger shoved the point of the shaft deep into the eye with all of his might driving it through the intruder's brain and out the back of its skull. Then just as quickly, he pulled the shaft back through the crack scraping blood and brain matter along the rough edges of the board. He heard the thump of the creatures face against the planking as its face bones were shattered, and he grimaced at the sickening sounds the rod made as it freed itself from the thing's skull and as the brain matter sloshed and slid down the outside of the barricade. The fowl stench coming from the horror made Roger's stomach lurch as he held back his urge to vomit. He needed to keep what little he had inside of him, as he hadn't eaten for days.

He listened as the body thudded to the ground outside then he backed away from the window silently waiting and paying attention to see if any others had heard the commotion. He felt weighed down with futility knowing all he could do was hope and wait. This was what his life had come down to; hoping and waiting.

After a few moments, satisfied all was clear he silently walked across the room to a tall dresser where he lit a match placing it against the wick of lone candle. This technique seemed to work well to provide minimal lighting without attracting unwanted attention. The last thing he needed was unwanted attention.

A calendar hung on the wall above the dresser showing the date in bold characters as February 14, Valentine's Day. Roger already knew it was Valentine's Day, but seeing the calendar just served to reinforce the importance of this day to him and to his sweet Amanda.

Roger crossed back to his rocker sitting, thinking about how quickly everything he knew to be true had gone completely down the crapper in a matter of just a few weeks. Again, he wondered how such a thing could have been possible.

Only a month and a half earlier he and his wife Amanda were toasting in the New Year and looking forward to the next year with great hopes and aspirations. They had been married about three years and were still madly in love. Roger's favorite expression of affection for Amanda was, "My heart is yours, for you alone." Amanda had never seemed to grow tired of hearing him say it.

They had decided this would be the year they would try to start a family. They had paid off both of their student loans had managed to scrape together enough money for a down payment on a starter home. Both of them were comfortably secure in their jobs and had agreed now was the time to start having children. They decided if they were to give their children all of the opportunities they possibly could, a two-income family would be required. Therefore, they would have to search for a good daycare or hire a nanny. They were already looking for the right match for their future needs even though Amanda hadn't even been pregnant yet.

Both Roger and Amanda were natural born planners. Many of their friends called them anal retentive, but they felt they were simply good managers. They believed in making a detailed outline of what direction they wanted their lives to take and then following the plan to the letter never deviating from their pathway and always heading forward with their final goals in mind.

Now sitting along in the near dark in a world gone to Hell, Roger was astonished at how quickly their clear-cut plans had fallen by the wayside practically overnight. Roger's Uncle Mike had always joked with him about Roger's obsession with planning. Mike would always say, "When things are going well and according to plan, start to worry. Because that means life is just waiting in the wings to jump out when you least expect it and kick you right square in the nuts." Uncle Mike was never one for pulling punches, and as it turned out, he had never spoken truer words in his life. Roger supposed his jovial uncle was now one of "them" as well.

Yes, the world Roger knew was gone. The life he had planned was over. Civilization had become obsolete. He didn't understand how or what happened, but he knew the results; he dealt with the results every day of his life.

One of Roger's major frustrations was he never actually found out exactly why the dead had decided to leave their graves, rise up and start walking the earth, feasting on the flesh of the living. He did, however, comprehend the world he loved was gone forever.

In addition to his being an obsessive planner, Roger was the type of person who tended to categorize and list things. The present situation was no exception. In Roger's organized mind, it seemed like he could place everyone in the world into one of three categories; they were either dead, missing or zombies.

Since the trouble started, Roger had also learned some new things about himself. He had never considered himself a strong or heroic type of person, but he quickly learned he had some previously unrecognized inner strength, which apparently made its presence known during times of crisis such as the present one.

When the zombies started roaming the streets, Roger found survivors behaved in several different ways (again he found himself categorizing). Some found inner strength required and rose to the occasion to fight for as long as was possible. This is what he surprisingly found himself doing.

Others broke down unable to cope. Many committed suicide, the most considerate being those who chose to blow off their own heads. This action alone guaranteed they wouldn't return as zombies. The others who chose to hanging, jumping off a bridge, or taking pills, in other words those who perhaps didn't think things through, simply died and then came back with a hunger for living human flesh.

One television news station reported a story about a man who had given up and hung himself by tying a rope around his neck throwing it over a beam in his garage then climbing on a chair which he subsequently kicked out from under him. Unfortunately, the man's neck didn't break, but he eventually choked to death. Shortly afterward, he re-awoke as a zombie still dangling from his neck in the garage unable to escape. The TV camera had filmed the creature twitching and swinging from its rope shortly before local volunteers blasted its head right off its jerking body.

Still others just shut down and went catatonic. It was common to see many of those types of people sitting in a stupor while the hordes of zombies surrounded them and devoured them. These were the strangest for Roger to comprehend. He saw one "cat" as he called them sitting in the middle of the street ripped apart and eaten alive without uttering a single cry or whimper. The man literally sat there and allowed himself to be a main course. Roger found this to be strange indeed, but then again, these were strange days.

Sadly for Roger Amanda had become one of the "cats" as well. He never would have expected her to react in that manner as she had always seemed strong and forceful, but he supposed after what she had been through he wasn't surprised.

It happened shortly after all the dead began dragging their rotting carcasses out of the ground. Up until a few weeks earlier, the living dead had been in the minority showing up in spotty locations around the city. The city police department, with the help of some civilian volunteers and hunters out for a good time, had been able to keep the zombies pretty much in check.

Once the news broke, most people wouldn't go anywhere unarmed. Everyone watched the news reports and learned quickly how to take the creatures down. The head seemed to be the key whether severing the head from the body with an ax or other sharp implement, or penetrating the brain with a sharp object such as a knife or a stick; or simply blowing the creatures' heads completely off with a 12 gauge, destroying the brain seemed to be just what the doctor ordered.

Another thing Roger noticed was the zombies weren't of the rapid moving variety pictured in many of the modern zombie-style horror films he had seen but seemed to be more in line with the slow, clumsy, spastically moving types depicted in the old George Romero flicks. This slowness initially proved to be helpful as it allowed everyone to manage the threat, at least for a while. Soon however, the sheer numbers of the lurching dead would turn the tide.

Although Roger had been aware of what was going on up until a few weeks ago, he and Amanda had continued to lead their lives as normally as possible, neither of them having ever seen an actual zombie other than those the saw on the television news broadcasts. The creatures seemed to be in isolated areas of the city and countryside and the authorities insisted they were properly controlling the.

As a precaution, Roger had purchased shotguns for both he and Amanda along with plenty of ammunition and had taken her to some farmland outside of the city to teach her how to shoot. She had proven to be a quick study, and Roger felt sure she would be able to defend herself if the need ever arose.

One day Roger came home from work and saw a note on the table from Amanda saying her cell phone was no longer getting service, but she had gotten a call on their landline from her mother who lived across town. She said her mother sounded hysterical and needed her help immediately. The note said she had headed right over to their house and would be home as soon as possible.

Roger took out his cell phone and saw he too had no service. He got a horrible feeling in the pit of his stomach; something was definitely wrong. Next, he tried the landline and saw that apparently all traditional phone service had gone down as well. Now he knew things had really started going bad.

Roger decided he had better head over to his in-laws' place and make sure they and Amanda were all right. He worked on the east side of town, and Amanda's parents lived on the west side. He hadn't encountered any problems on his way home from work and hoped this would be the case as he headed west.

He ran to his car shotgun in hand and unfortunately, as he drove, he noticed the west side of town painted a completely different picture than his daily commute. That side of town proved to be zombie central.

Rounding a corner just a few blocks from his and Amanda's home, he witnessed several zombies shot in the street by locals. Three men dressed in hunting gear were standing at on the corner with their backs toward each other pointing in opposite directions, firing away as a steady stream of zombies stumbled toward them. It was like watching a video game. Bang and the top of one zombie's head flew through the air. Bang and another zombie fell to the ground.

The men were all laughing and drinking beer between kills and having themselves a great old time. That was until a group of about thirty zombies staggered spasmodically from a nearby building overpowering the men by force of the numbers, falling on them and ripping them to shreds. Roger had to look away in order to keep control of his car while again struggling not to vomit.

As he traveled, things got progressively worse. In one neighborhood, he saw several residents overpowered by zombies then eaten alive. The creatures were gnawing on limbs ripped off the victims. Some of the wounded lay bleeding to death on the street screaming in pain as more zombies approached to finish them off. Roger wanted to stop and help but realized it was futile. In addition, he knew if things had gotten this bad this fast, he had better get to Amanda as soon as possible.

A block away from his destination, Roger saw several zombies clumsily shambling down the middle of the street directly in the path of his car. He did the only thing he could think of to do and pressed the gas pedal to the floor. Roger plowed right into the pack sending bodies flying in all directions. Looking in his rear view mirror, he saw them fall back to the ground breaking into pieces with arms and legs flying in several directions. Even without arms or legs, the reanimated corpses that survived still squirmed on the ground like worms driven by an insatiable need for human flesh.

A few moments later, Roger pulled in front of his in-law's home and saw Amanda's car parked in the driveway with the driver's door standing open. He pulled in behind grabbed his shotgun and headed for her car fearing he might find her dead inside. She wasn't there, but her shotgun was which told Roger she must have panicked and ran right for her parents' home leaving the gun behind.

As Roger approached the front door of the house, he heard a groaning and moaning sound from his left and saw an old woman in a housecoat dragging her wounded right leg and lurching directly toward him her arms outstretched. He recognized her as Mrs. Wilson the old woman who lived next door. He could immediately see she was no longer the sweet old grandmother he had known, but was now one of them. Without hesitation, he lifted the gun pulled the trigger and blew poor dead old Mrs. Wilson's head right off of her shoulders. Her decapitated body continued to take one more step forward before dropping to the ground with a thud.

Roger looked around to make sure there were no more former neighbors to deal with and for the moment, there were no others. He turned and noticed the front door of his in-law's home was standing ajar. Roger knew this wouldn't be good.

Slowly he entered the front hall of the large center-hall colonial style home and heard a sound, which sent chills down his spine. To his right coming from the living room he heard moaning as well as a sickening slurping sound like he imagined might come from a group of wild pigs. Being careful not to make a sound shotgun at the ready Roger slowly entered the living room.

His stomach lurched at the sight awaiting him. His young brother-in-law Jared was kneeling on the floor over top of the prone body of Roger's mother-in-law Celia, Jared's own mother. The boy was covered in blood from head to toe and was gorging on her entrails, which he apparently had ripped from her stomach. The serpentine intestines flapped through the air spewing blood in all directions as the hideous thing feasting on her playfully allowing the slimy tube-like organs to slide through his fingers.

As if that were not bad enough, Roger could see the woman was still alive, and though unconscious, she was twitching uncontrollably as if moments away from death. Again, without hesitation, Roger lifted the shotgun and separated Jared from his head as the blast sent the zombie flying across the living room and splattering against the far wall.

No sooner had Roger reloaded the gun then his mother-in-law or what once had been his mother-in-law started crawling toward him staring at him with dead eyes bloody drool oozing from her lips as her innards sloshed along the hardwood floor behind her. Roger was shocked to see how quickly she had become one of them it was no wonder they were multiplying so rapidly. With one more quick blast of the shotgun, he managed to obliterate her head, leaving a large hole in the living room floor as well.

Regaining his composure Roger heard banging and scraping sounds coming from the second floor. Taking the stairs two at a time he entered the upstairs hall to find his father-in-law Bob now one of the living dead banging ineptly on the door to what Roger knew was once Amanda's bedroom back when she was a little girl.

Upon hearing Roger's approach, the zombie turned and headed straight for him. Roger aimed the gun at the creature's head pulled the trigger but the gun didn't fire probably because he had forgotten to reload it in his haste. He did the only thing he could think of and swung the gun barrel at the zombie's skull. Roger heard a cracking sound as the creature fell to the floor down but not out as it started slowly crawling in his direction. He realized he must have broken the thing's neck because its movements were jerky and its head dragged along the floor its jaws snapping instinctively in search for flesh.

As it got within a foot of Roger, he grabbed the stock of his shotgun and drove the both barrels downward through the top of the father-in-law thing's skull like a knife through a melon as blood and brain matter shot upward. With a grunting sound, the monster ceased its forward motion twitched a few times then was dead, really dead this time on the hall floor.

Roger went to the bedroom door banging frantically calling out to his Amanda. At first she didn't reply. Eventually he heard her sobs coming from just inside the door and then heard her unlocking the lock, which had succeeded in keeping her alive. Roger opened the door and Amanda collapsed into his arms breaking down hysterically screaming and crying.

Keeping her eyes shielded from the gory sight of her once father's skull crushed in the hall Roger guided Amanda down the stairs. Once on the first floor he again protected her from the carnage in the living room turning her away though he was already certain she had already seen much too much on that eventful day.

Cautiously looking out the front door to make sure the coast was clear; Roger picked up Amanda and carried her to his car placing her gently in the passenger's seat strapping the seatbelt securely around her. Keeping himself covered with the shotgun, eyes scanning the street he went back to her car and picked up her shotgun tossing in the backseat of his car as he climbed inside and secured him seatbelt.

He knew he had to find somewhere safe for them to lay low. Judging by the way this plague seemed to be spreading and how close it was now to their own home, he felt he might not be able to make it back there safely. Locking all the doors and securing the windows Roger sped away in search of a less vulnerable location.

As luck would have it he found a two story warehouse turned loft apartment only a few blocks from his in-laws' home, and there didn't seem to be any zombies anywhere near it. He noticed someone had covered the windows on both floors with boards to prevent any zombies from getting inside but the front door was standing open. He got out of the car leaving Amanda locked safely inside and quickly entered the property making sure the apartment was clear of any unwanted activity.

He went from room to room on the first floor and then headed up the stairs to check the second floor as well. The place had four bedrooms upstairs each of which was empty; that was until he got to the last one. Upon entering the last bedroom, Roger smelled an ungodly stench and found the body of a man most likely the former resident of the apartment. The corpse was headless, its brains splattered on the wall behind it and it was sitting in a pool of blood on the floor with a note next to it.

The message had obviously been written in haste and under extreme conditions as it was barely legible. The note read "I been bitten. I near dead. I don't wanna come back. As one of those things." Next to the corpse was a high-powered rifle, which the man had used to do the deed. Roger was grateful the man had chosen to remove his own head saving him the trouble.

As Roger left the room, he closed and locked the door behind him. He had to get back to Amanda. He raced down the stairs and out the front door to find Amanda was still safe in the car sitting and staring into space. Looking around to make sure no other zombies had arrived; Roger opened the door and lifted Amanda out of the car. He carried her into the living room placing her safely on a sofa and then returned to close and secure the door from any other potential invaders.

Roger realized although the zombies were the major threat at the moment from what he had witnessed today, the very fabric of civilization was breaking down around him, and he would have to be wary of everyone the living and the undead.

Now many weeks later instead of getting better, Amanda seemed to be getting worse with each passing day. She was becoming more uncommunicative and distant. She had stopped eating and drinking several days ago, and he couldn't seem to be able to force food or water into her. It was as if she had given up and wanted to die. Her ill-fated behavior was affecting Roger as well causing him to lose his resolve. He found himself falling into a depression which worsened daily and from which he might not recover.

Amanda had been the love of his life and to watch her fading away right before his eyes with him helpless to do anything about it was more than he believed he could take. He found it strange even though the world as he knew it had ended, as long as he had Amanda, he believed he could deal with anything. Now he seemed to be losing her as well. Without her, he doubted he would want to go on.

Roger sat in the rocker looking across the room at the calendar displaying February 14. He recalled how this was going to be a special Valentine's Day for him and Amanda. He was going to buy a beautiful bracelet for her she had been admiring. Then he planned they would go out for dinner come home and make love, and perhaps this would have been the night they made a baby. However, now Roger realized this was not to be, not this Valentine's Day and not ever again. There would be no baby for Roger and Amanda, no babies for anyone.

He decided he should check on Amanda and see how she was doing. He walked the stairs to her second floor bedroom and opened the door to find her curled up in the fetal position on the bed. Roger approached her and gently touched her cheek, which felt as cold as ice to him. A second later her eyes flew open covered in a grey film. She sat up in bed her emaciated form visible under the nightgown, which now hung from her bony shoulders. Long gone was the look of loving affection also gone was the catatonic stare, both replaced by a savage look of hunger Roger knew was reserved for the warm-blooded walking lunch wagons formerly known as the human race. He realized he had just made it to the top of the menu.

Roger backed away slowly from the bed, turned and ran into an adjacent bathroom slamming the door behind him. He stood in the bathroom slamming his fists against his head not knowing what to do next. His once beloved wife Amanda was now scratching and clawing at the bathroom door. No, this was no longer his wife. Amanda was gone. All that remained was a lifeless reanimated corpse, which wanted nothing better than to eat him alive.

He sat down hard on the toilet lid his head in his hands and cried, as he had never done before. His mind was on the verge of breaking he knew it and he simply didn't care.

Without his Amanda, there was no life. Then he realized he had been kidding himself all this time because, even if Amanda was alive and healthy, there was no more life for them, no more life at all. It was futile; it was over.

Roger stood and slowly walked to the bathroom door took a deep breath grabbed door handle saying, "Amanda, honey?" He slowly turned the knob and said, "I love you." Finally, he pulled the door open and saw the thing, which had once been Amanda standing outside the bathroom its white night gown covered in filth.

He looked directly into the zombie's dead eyes and said, "My heart is yours, for you alone. Happy Valentine's Day, Baby." With that, the creature charged into the bathroom sunk her claw-like fingers into Roger's chest, pulled out his still beating heart and began her feast.

BORDELLO OF THE BIZARRE

Walter awoke in a stupor, finding himself in an unfamiliar place and for some reason not completely in charge of all of his faculties. His head throbbed with a weightiness he couldn't quite describe other than it simply felt thick, as if his brain was swollen inside his skull. He was having trouble focusing, and it seemed like he was experiencing his surroundings from the bottom of a deep murky swimming pool. Each of his senses seemed like they were equally sluggish, like he was under the influence of some type of drug, some nasty stuff. Although partaking of such drugs was common to Walter Anderson, especially when it helped him to deal with certain unpleasant memories, he couldn't recall taking anything recently.

He realized he was sitting on a curb at a crossroad intersection of two streets in what appeared to be some type of small town, somewhere. Where, exactly he had absolutely no idea. He felt perhaps he should recognize the town, the look and feel reminding him somewhat of his hometown where he lived as a child until the age of ten, but yet it was significantly different. He supposed every small town everywhere in the country was in some way similar to every other small town.

He was surprised to discover he couldn't hear a single sound. Surely he should have heard some sort of activity, birds chirping, people talking, dogs barking, car engines running, something. Although he could neither see nor hear any people, he had assumed there must be someone in the town somewhere. He wondered if perhaps he had been stricken deaf. He lifted his right hand in front of his face and snapped his fingers. He heard the snap although the sound was dull, less like a snap and more like a light thud, as if the air around him was so heavy it wouldn't permit the carrying of sounds.

He took a deep breath and noticed the air didn't feel quite right to him. It was warmer than normal, perhaps bordering on hot and it felt very thick in his lungs like it had some sort of substance to it. It wasn't quite the same as heaviness of humid air since it was definitely dry, but it nonetheless felt strangely weighted.

Slowly, he tried to get to his feet immediately noticing he was a bit wobbly and uncertain of his balance. He also observed the strange heavy air made it difficult for him to maneuver quickly causing him to move in slow motion. He carefully took a step or two and felt as though his legs were knee deep in a thick quagmire. Perhaps he was in the midst of a dream. He didn't believe so; he believed he was wide-awake but then recalled how often had he felt he was awake while he was in fact, in a deep sleep. Maybe that was it. Perhaps this was a dream. He took two fingers of his right hand and pinched the skin of his left wrist between his fingernails.

"Ouch!" Walter shouted, the shout sounding like a faraway muffled voice to his ears. Again, he thought about the thick sound unfriendly air. He imagined his sound waves getting a fraction of an inch from his lips then scattered about in the gelatinous atmosphere of this strange place.

He stood on the street at the corner slowly looking around and trying to get some idea as to where exactly he was and perhaps more importantly, why he was here in the first place. He also wondered what he should do next. As he moved his head from side to side, he heard a humming and whining sound deep inside his head perhaps inside his brain, as if the air moving past his skull was doing so at an incredibly high speed. It reminded him of sitting in a parked car with the window open while another car raced by. Then an incredible piercing pain began to develop within his skull. It started out small, barely noticeable and before long blossomed into inconceivable agony. He put his hands up to his ears hunching over while taking another stumbling step away from the curb. Then as quickly as it had occurred, the sound vanished, as did the pain and the silence returned.

"What the Hell was that?" he wondered aloud, again hearing his words disintegrate into a muddled jumble in the air around him.

Walter lifted his head and slowly turned to determine what he could discover about his new surroundings. His father had always told him "Walter, before you can figure out where you are going, you had better know where you are." He understood the double meaning of the phrase and appreciated the folksiness if not corniness of the expression.

"So," he said, "Before I plan on going somewhere, I had better figure out where exactly I am."

He looked to his left and saw what at first appeared to be a familiar main street, very similar to his childhood hometown, which he recalled had been built on the side of a hill. The street headed upward at a steep angle ever narrowing in perspective until it seemed to end at a point far away at the horizon line. There was no movement or activity on this street and upon closer examination, Walter believed this wasn't really a street at all but simply some sort of image like a painting or photograph of what a street would look like. But it wasn't exactly a picture either. He could see it wasn't real yet there it was right in front of him. It seemed to exist in only two dimensions as if someone was projecting the image onto the air itself. As thick as this air felt, Walter believed such a thing might actually be possible.

He wondered if he crossed the street and tried to touch the image if it might ripple like the surface of a pond when struck by a rock. Or maybe his hand would sink into and then pass through the image like he was dunking his hand into some sort of jelly. Then the cautious part of his brain took over, and he questioned if maybe his hand would simply go right through the representation into some alternate dimension or something of that nature. He also wondered what would happen to his hand if it did go though. Would he pull back a stump where his hand had been? Would he bleed to death as his lifeblood pumped from the severed limb? Or would the stump be cauterized by the same inter-dimensional force supporting the street image? Apparently, there was a lot for him to consider. Walter decided now might not be the best time to try such an experiment.

Putting his thoughts about the strange projection aside, he looked in front of him and saw the street heading in that direction continued for about a half a block or so then seemed to end abruptly, not the type of dead end one would find when a street encountered a building or anything of that sort; it just ended. In fact, everything beyond the street ended like someone had taken a giant eraser and wiped out all of reality beyond that point.

He chanced a glance behind him, and as he expected, the same scenario played out with the street ending a block or so back with literally nothing beyond there whatsoever. He stood in the silence for a moment, reluctant to look in his last remaining direction out of fear it too might prove not to exist as well. Then what would he do?

Cautiously and with great reluctance, he turned to look to the last remaining direction, his right. He found he was looking downward at the continuation of the hilly main street, but this time it was no longer a two dimensional image; it was an actual street which seemed to lead into some sort of downtown shopping district. Walter didn't know why he believed it was a shopping district. There was nothing about the area to suggest it; he simply had a "knowing" deep in is mind this street was a market of sorts. He also knew he wasn't familiar with this sort of shopping area.

The city where Walter lived had many well-known chain stores, restaurants, and fast food places as well as a nice collection of local businesses, which all had one thing in common: they looked like places to shop. They all had brightly colored signs and recognizable logos. This area didn't have the same feel. He was certain things might be sold on this street, but he suspected the things sold here were going to be quite different from anything he could buy back home.

Walter noticed the street itself was in excellent condition, smooth with what appeared to be a fresh coat of black top and a series of well-maintained bright white wood framed clapboard row houses lined the street. The buildings may have once been residences converted to businesses giving the area a quaint and unique appearance. He couldn't wait to see what sort of products these stores had to offer.

Clumsily, he began to walk heavy-footed down the street breathing irregularly in the unpleasant air. As he passed the point where the streets intersected and was on the downhill main street, something disturbing happened. Right before his eyes the street started to narrow and was soon no wider than an alley losing its smooth appearance. The street developed huge cracks and faded from its deep black color to various shades of gray. Large pot holes formed as the blacktop surface sunk downward while at the same time in other sections of the street complete chunks of asphalt rose up as if jack hammered sticking up at odd angles. Walter couldn't believe his eyes now understanding why there were likely no cars on this street. Driving an automobile down this horrible alley would be impossible. He stepped up off the street onto the pavement, which although broken and worn, seemed to be safer to navigate than the street.

He looked at the once lovely homes to see they too had changed drastically. Gone was the shiny coat of white paint, replaced by grayed and yellowed paint-chipped coating on what appeared to be broken down shacks in dire need of repair. The first building he came wasn't open for business. The front door of the building stood shut and behind the cracked glass window, a well-worn "Closed" sign hung askew between the cloudy glass and a ripped and filthy cloth blind. The stores main display window was also murky in appearance and likewise cracked at various spots. Walter noticed spider webs covered the window and doors and he thought for a moment he saw huge rat scurry under the wooden landing at the entrance. Walter was disgusted by the condition of this place, but curiosity got the better of him and he wanted to see what sorts of items it sold.

Approaching the window he squinted to see and was shocked to notice several armless female mannequins completely naked displayed in the window. Looking closer he observed they didn't appear to be constructed from plaster or plastic or whatever materials were generally used to make mannequins. Instead, they seemed to be covered with a material resembling actual flesh.

As he continued to look at them, the mannequins began to change. The skin started to decay, rotting right in front of him. As he looked at their heads, he noticed their hair started falling out in clumps and their teeth begin to loosen and fall from their receding gums. Maggots bored holes through the mottled gray flesh. Walter realized there were no joint lines on these mannequins where the head met the torso or where the torso met the lower body. In horror, Walter understood these things were not mannequins but were actual dead female bodies.

At the place where the arms should have met the shoulders jagged bones jutted from rotten flesh showing where someone had ripped off the arms. Flies slammed against the inside of the window trying to get to Walter, first a few then several then hundreds. Soon he couldn't see inside the window because thousands of flies covered the the glass.

Walter backed away in horror and slowly struggled down the street away from the ghastly sight. Suddenly he had no desire to see what other sorts of things might be for sale on this horrific street. He struggled to move down the sidewalk away from the store and although making progress he moved at what seemed like a snail's pace.

After an interminable amount of time seemed to pass, Walter found himself standing in front of another business. The building housing this enterprise also appeared well worn and in disrepair. It didn't have a picture type window as the first horrible building had and still resembled a house. On the inside of the windows, Walter saw thick velvet-red colored drapes which he assumed must obscure most light from entering the building and provide privacy. A simple red light shone above the front door.

The door stood open, and as Walter approached it, he saw he was correct about no light entering the place since it was in complete darkness other than the minimal light entering from the open door. Standing directly in front of the doorway he saw there was a service counter at the back of the room about twelve feet inside of the door. Someone stood behind the counter, but he couldn't make out the person's appearance. Walter was so excited to have finally seen another living being in this strange place, without forethought he walked into the room and directly to the counter.

Approaching the counter, he noticed its filthy condition, even in the minimal lighting. It was a typical wooden and glass sales counter but most of the paint had worn off revealing some of the original shabby varnished finish underneath. The glass in the front of the display case appeared pitted and cracked. Inside the case, Walter saw a collection of what looked like adult toys, dildos and such coated with spider webs and other filth. The devices seemed to not have been fabricated of rubber or plastic but of human flesh, and like the skin on the mannequins he had seen earlier, these tools were gray and mottled in appearance. Staring at one particular sexual implement, he saw a worm-like creature crawling out of the hole at the head of the shaft. His stomach turned with revolution.

Walter looked up to see the clerk, standing behind the counter, a woman, who looked at him through hooded uninterested eyes. The woman was of the type Walter would describe as "hard" or perhaps more appropriately the phrase "road hard and put away wet" came to mind. Her hair was bleached blonde with long dark roots. Her face was haggard and wrinkled. A cigarette hung low from the right corner of her lips, which she had smeared with far too much lipstick. She had apparently applied her make-up in the haphazard manor of someone who was drunk, high on drugs or simply didn't care. She closed her right eye to shield it from the rising smoke from the cigarette as Walter had seen so many smokers do in his lifetime. Her flesh seemed to hang on her bones as her emaciated frame scarcely held up her soiled and worn flower-print sundress on her shoulders. Walter tried to avoid staring at her sagging breasts which dangled like wind socks, visible through the low opening of her dress. But it was like a train wreck and he couldn't seem to avert his gaze.

"What can I do for you?" the woman inquired. Her reply gave Walter a strange sensation in the pit of his stomach. He felt as if for some unknown reason this woman was expecting him and not at all surprised to see him standing there.

Walter ignored his uneasy feeling and replied, "Ah, yes. This may sound rather odd. But where am I? What is this place?

"This place?" The woman replied, "Why this place is a bordello of sorts."

"A bordello?" Walter asked, surprised by her direct reply.

"A brothel, a whore house. You know . . . a bordello."

"Of course, I know what a bordello is!" Walter said. "It's just this doesn't look like any bordello I have ever seen."

She replied slowly and deliberately in a tone Walter took as suspicious and perhaps knowing, "I don't believe you've ever seen the inside of a bordello, Mr. Anderson. Have you?"

"Well, of course, I've never been to a bordello," Walter answered then with sudden realization he asked, "Hey, wait a minute. How did you know my name? I never told you my name."

The woman ignored his question and simply replied in that same unhurried monotone, "I don't believe you'd have any interest in what we have to offer here, Mr. Anderson. Your tastes appear to go, shall we say, to the much younger cuisine." The cigarette bounced up and down in the corner of her mouth as she spoke, ashes falling to the countertop.

"What are you suggesting?" Walter Anderson replied in surprise. "You know nothing about me. I've never been in this place before in my life."

"Perhaps not, but we've been expecting you for quite some time," she replied, taking out the cigarette and blowing a smoke ring, which Walter stopped to watch in awe as it slowly ascended upward before eventually dissipating. Then he recalled what she had said.

"Expecting me? Why in Hell would a whorehouse in God knows where be expecting me?" Walter asked. "And where in Hell is this place, anyway?"

"Where in Hell indeed," the haggard woman replied with a snide grin followed by a deep rumbling smokers cough. A plop of crimson spittle landed on the glass counter top where it beaded. "Tell me, Walter, what's the last thing you remember before waking up in our fair city?"

Walter stood and thought for a moment then replied, "I can't really recall anything. I don't remember what I was doing just before I ended up here. I think someone drugged me and dumped me here. That's what I think. Maybe you were part of the whole scheme."

Again, the woman ignored his comment saying, "Poor, poor Walter. Perhaps the trauma you took to the head scattered your memory. It happens sometimes. Allow me to refresh things for you."

She reached under the counter and pulled up a notebook flipping it open to the first page. She read with disinterest, "Your name is Walter Anderson. You are a happily married middle-aged father living in a desirable suburban subdivision in Pennsylvania. You are considered one of the pillars of your community, being a successful local businessman, a member of the country club, a deacon in your church, a coach on the little league team and a scout leader. Does that all seem familiar to you?"

Walter thought for a moment and replied, "Yes, that sounds right to me, but what does it have to do with all of this?"

She replied, again looking down at her notes and turning the page, "Well, let me see here. Oh, this isn't very good. It appears there's a darker side to the good Mr. Anderson; one you managed to keep hidden from everyone at least for a while. This was the Walter Anderson who enjoyed having his way, sexually, with small children."

"Nonsense!" Walter demanded. "That's all a pack of lies drummed up by people who were obviously jealous of my success."

"Spare me, Walter," the woman replied, "You see, you have no secrets here. That innocent plea is the sort of thing, which should have saved for your trial. But you never made it to trial, did you?"

Walter looked confused, "I don't know. I don't remember. The last thing I remember is they had arrested me and charged me with those ridiculous crimes. I made bail and was back trying to get my life back to normal."

"Yes, you were trying to live your life," she interrupted, "but according to these notes things were far from normal. Several young boys and girls came forward claiming you had sexually molested them. The police had their sworn statements and managed to find your DNA present in several of the cases. Your wife left you and filed for divorce. She would certainly have gotten the house, the cars, and most of your other possessions. You had no children, which is probably a good thing. Perhaps if you had your own children, you might have kept the abuse at home, so to speak. Not necessarily a better option but perhaps the lesser of two evils."

"Ridiculous!" Walter interrupted. "They had nothing on me. It was all circumstantial evidence."

"So you thought," She continued, "until they found the decomposed body of little Jillian Wilkins buried under your back porch. That wasn't a very smart move, Walter, burying the girl so close to home, not very smart at all."

Memories started returning to Walter. He recalled how he had been doing a good job of staying several steps ahead of the law and had hired a top-notch attorney to plead his case. He didn't really care about his wife leaving, the old sow, and he believed his attorney could get all of the charges dropped.

"Yep," she explained, "finding the little girl was the straw that broke the pervert's back so to speak." She reached under the counter and pulled out a newspaper. "Would you like to read tomorrow morning's front page headline?"

Walter stood stunned unable to speak. As the wretched woman opened the newspaper and held it up for him to read the headline screaming, "Local Civic Leader Commits Suicide," with Walter's picture directly under it and the story to follow.

"What?" Walter asked. "What's this?"

The woman said, "Allow me to paraphrase to give you the gist of the article. It says you fled the state after police had found the young girl's body under your back porch. There was a massive police manhunt underway, and they

didn't particularly care if they brought you back dead or
alive. Apparently, you checked into some fleabag hotel. You
even used your own credit card, which again wasn't very
smart, but by then you simply no longer cared. Next, you
went into your hotel room and wrote a long letter
confessing everything and saying how sorry you were even
though we both know you weren't. Then you stuck the
barrel of a 38-caliber handgun into your mouth and blew
your brains out. That's probably why you're having the
lapse in memory. That sort of thing is nasty business."

Walter stood motionless, in shock, unable to speak. The
woman explained, "You see, Walter, suicide is frowned
upon in the universe. You may recall such an act is
considered a mortal sin. By the way, the disgusting things
you did to those poor children, those happened to be
mortal sins as well. Your antics earned you a one-way
ticket to Hell. Do not pass go; do not collect two hundred
dollars."

As the woman closed the notebook, Walter noticed she
had scars running vertically along her wrists. "Your
wrists," he said. "You committed suicide as well?"

"Sure did," the woman replied, "and I did it out of
depression. I didn't have quite as vile a history as you did.
You see, I was a drug addict and a prostitute. I suppose
that's why I ended up here in this bordello. I did get a
promotion, however; now I'm the madam."

"But I wasn't a prostitute." Walter inquired, "What am I
doing here in a brothel? I don't belong here."

"On the contrary, this is exactly where you belong. And
as I mentioned we've been waiting for you to arrive and
looking forward to it for some time."

"I couldn't care less about what you were waiting for.
I'm out of here!" Walter said turning to leave the building
only to find after turning around he was unable to move;
his view was now focused out onto the street. The area
outside was no longer empty but was crowded and busy
with creatures moving about. "Creatures" was the correct
word because they certainly weren't human. They looked
like gargoyles he saw on old buildings or perhaps demons
he saw depicted in horror movies. Whatever they were, they
certainly weren't human.

As he stood unable to move, he heard the sound of light feet walking toward him out of the darkened area of the front room. Two gorgeous naked female legs in high heels walked with jerky movements toward him out of the darkness. They didn't have a body attached, only legs and the bottom part of a woman, no torso, with no private parts showing and nothing above the waist. The legs stopped directly in front of him. Walter looked down into what he expected to be the severed remains of where the body had once been located, but was shocked to see the area covered with flesh. Suddenly a slit opened in the center of the area and Walter saw he was looking at the thing's vagina.

As he watch the lips of the ghastly thing started to move and the foul odor of rotten eggs, dead vegetation and road kill emerged from the opening while the thing spoke a series of sounds resembling some sort of foreign language. He couldn't comprehend how this vagina thing was speaking to him. Somehow, Walter was able to understand the meaning of the language and in his mind heard the thing say, "Hello, Walter Anderson. Welcome to our miserable little corner of Hell. You won't enjoy the eternity in store for you in our little house of oddities."

Next, he looked down and to his right and saw a hand emerging from the dark side of the room, dragging itself into the light using its fingers to pull its arm behind it. As it came fully into the light, Walter saw it was only an arm, nothing else. It dragged itself over to his leg, and as he looked down, he saw the thing using American Sign Language as he had seen deaf people use. Although in life, he couldn't understand sign, he again understood everything the hand was saying. "You may have used children as toys in your life Walter, but now you will become a toy for those creatures you see outside." The hand grabbed his ankle and tried to crawl up his leg.

A few seconds later he heard a thump, thump sound and saw a female torso loosely clothed in a lacy see-through top coming out of the darkness walking on its hands hanging on long arms below the point where the torso ended. The thing had no head and at the stump of its neck, a bone jutted upward, maggots crawling among the area where the head had once been.

Walter felt the world around him start to fade away as behind him he heard the woman at the desk say, "Welcome to Hell, Walter Anderson. Soon you'll find your rightful place among my special odd collection of pleasure givers." It was the last thing he heard before collapsing into blackness.

Sometime later, Walter awoke in darkness. He couldn't feel his hands or feet and couldn't move. His head and mouth ached; feeling like some sort of sharp implement had ripped open his mouth. He could see across the darkness of the room to the service counter where the tired haggard madam sat smoking and reading a magazine.

He heard a grunting sound and saw a horrible hunched creature drag itself through the front door. The woman greeted the being saying, "Welcome, Bezelack. We haven't seen you here in a while."

Standing in front of the counter was a deformed demon, perhaps only four feet tall. It stood naked and covered from head to toe in sweat and filth. The air in the room reeked with its vile stench. Its muscular arms hung down to the floor and led to huge hands with long razor sharp claws. From between its legs jutted an enormous penis-like appendage at least two feet long and four inches in diameter, dragging on the floor. The demon replied in a gravelly voice, "I took a break from here for a while. I got tired of the same old thing. I'm looking for something new, something different."

She smiled down at the obscene creature and said, "Well, today is your lucky day. I think I have just what you were looking for." Then she shouted, "Can somebody please wheel out Mr. Anderson?" Walter was shocked and unable to comprehend what was happening. What did she mean by, "Wheel out Mr. Anderson?"

The demon looked into the darkness in anticipation, waiting to see what new oddity the madam had in store for him. He heard the squeaking of wheels as a cart entered the room, pulled forward out of the darkness by the two-legged vagina thing.

Sitting atop the cart was a rectangular open-sided metal frame. Suspended by razor wire in the center of the frame was the living alert head of Walter Anderson. His eyes darted back and forth, as sweat gathered on his brow. His mouth hung wide open forced by four hooks, two on top and two on the bottom piercing the insides of his cheeks and stretching his mouth into a gaping position. On the sides of the metal box were two gripper handles for the customers to solidly grasp and lift the box. The demonic creature reached out and firmly took hold of the handles in its claws. Somewhere inside of Walter Anderson's brain, he understood and silently screamed.

"Enjoy yourself, Bezelack, for as long as you choose, and if you're satisfied be sure to spread the word. You see Mr. Anderson will be here with us for the pleasure of you and all your friends for a very, very long time."

DEER GAP

"And God said, 'Let us make man in our image, after our likeness: and let them have dominion over the fish of the sea, and over the fowl of the air, and over the cattle, and over all the earth, and over every creeping thing that creeps on the earth.'" —Genesis 1:26

A shabby black 2000 Pontiac Firebird sailed along the narrow two-lane country road at a speed much too fast for the wet conditions. A sticker reading "Love Me, Love My Mullet" hung askew on the rear bumper, its corners turned up and peeling. Lynyrd Skynyrd's song *That Smell* exploded from the thundering oversized speakers as the bass pounded mercilessly from the rear, practically rattling the windows from their frames.

Leon tried to focus to the best of his ability while his eyes darted back and forth and his hand pounded the steering wheel in anger and frustration. When the song spoke about the smell of death surrounding the subject of the tune, Leon looked at the dashboard for a moment in amazement convinced the CD player was speaking specifically to him. He shook his head for an instant rattling the idea out of his mind. He had to clear his head.

This was how Leon always worked out his problems, by driving his nine-year-old Firebird at high speeds out on the open road. He was a hard living, hard drinking high school dropout having left school in 2000 shortly after getting his driver's license. He bought the used Pontiac with money he saved from his part time job at the local "Barf Burger" as he was fond of calling it. The Firebird was the love of his life. Lately however, it was becoming as frayed around the edges as Leon was.

So now in 2010, he found himself laid off from yet another entry-level job at the local foundry with his unemployment benefits about a month from running out as well. Yet somehow, he always managed to scrape together money for beer and weed. No one could say Leon Trakowsky didn't have his priorities in order.

He had completely lost track of time and hadn't been paying attention to where he was going. He looked at himself in the rearview mirror and saw his eyes were red from drinking, crying or both as he absently flicked the long mullet hair hanging down on his neck. He could scarcely remember the events of the past twenty minute drive as he had focused so intently on the horrible events of the previous few hours.

He couldn't believe how his life had changed so much since last night. He recalled fleeing the rundown apartment he shared with his girlfriend Jolene in Ashton, Pennsylvania at around three in the morning. He recalled heading north on Rt. 51 past the site of what was once the Coogan Coal Mine where an old mine fire had been burning out of control underground since the sixties. He must have driven right past the turn in the burned out town of Cantrainia where Rt. 51 hung a sharp left heading over to Mount Carroll.

He realized he had already passed through the village of Marista and was now heading north on Route 32. At this rate, it wouldn't be long until he would enter the town of Catswhisker and shortly after that Brumfield, home of Brumfield State University. Leon knew this would never do; he needed more country road. He had to stay away from big towns. He had to get his head screwed on straight, and driving on the open road was the only way he knew to accomplish what he needed to do.

Then he recalled somewhere up ahead just before he got to Catswhisker there was another road, which would take him over to Rt. 44 and passing through the area known as Deer Gap. It would give him another five or ten miles of open country road to think. Then once he got over to Rt. 44 he could continue north to Danesville, sneak through town and up to the interstate. From there he could head west then continue to work his way north through New York State toward the Canadian border. He had no idea what he would do when he got there. He heard these days you definitely needed either a passport or some sort of border pass to cross into Canada and he had neither. He supposed he'd have to figure it out later. For now, he was just moving. Leon kept his eyes peeled for the Deer Gap turnoff.

As he drove he recounted how he and Jolene had been having another one of their typical knock down drag out fights, usually not a major problem, but tonight this one had ended very badly.

He just could never figure out that crazy woman. He had always bought her anything he could afford, which might not have been much, but he tried, you had to give him that. He tolerated most of her wacky ideas even her latest Wicca or Witchcraft thing she had been into so heavily for the past year or two. That was a tough one for him to accept, and surprisingly she had stuck with it for a long time.

Usually Jolene would get into some new idea for a month or so. Then she'd dump it in search of something else. But this earth mother nature earth-child thing she was into had not only hung around for a long time but had seemed to intensify more every day. She really believed all this witchcraft mumbo jumbo. It was like some weird religious cult or something and she was hooked on it big time. Hell, she even started calling herself a Wicca High Priestess telling him with the proper spells she could control the very forces of nature, the ditzy broad.

She was also getting more difficult for Leon to control of late and less caring about what he thought about much of anything. It was almost as if she only kept him around to provide her with weed and booze and the occasional tumble in the hay. The idea didn't bother him too much. As long as he had somewhere to put little Leon from time to time, he could tolerate quite a lot.

However, lately she started talking a lot about having a baby. Was she nuts? The last thing Leon wanted or needed was a snot-nosed little rug-rat running around, especially one he might end up having to support for eighteen or more years. One time he even caught her dancing around the bedroom casting what she said was some kind of fertility spell.

He also believed if she ever did manage to become pregnant, she might drop him like a hot potato and take off with the bun in the oven. Then later she'd likely send him the bill in the form of eighteen years of child support. Maybe she'd just run off and join a tribe of those crazy Amazon witches. He knew that was how many of those types thought these days. Lots of them believed the only use for a man was to provide the seed for offspring; then once the deed was done, men really didn't serve much purpose for them anymore. Leon may not have been a high school graduate, but he did watch a ton TV and knew a lot more than most people might think.

Leon and Jolene's relationship had always been a stormy one, and lately it had gotten much stormier especially during the past six months or so. From time to time, they'd fight about almost anything. She'd hit him and throw things at him on occasion, and he might have to knock her around now and then but nothing to get too worked up about; that was until tonight.

The evening had started out like any other night. He had put away a half of case of Yuengling or "Ying-Yang" as he and his buds liked to call it. He had also smoked a few bones before he and Jolene had a good session of "hide the salami." At least it was good for him.

He figured something must be wrong with her maybe just some weird chick thing. Lately she had become distant and uninterested. He figured it was something she'd get over on her own, and as long as he was getting his own ashes hauled, he could wait as long as it took her to get back to normal.

Then somehow things had gone south in a hurry. After leaving the bedroom last night they went to the kitchen so she could make them a snack, which was their usual routine. Jolene was wearing her sheer white nightgown leaving very little to the imagination. Checking out the merchandise, Leon had started to think shortly he and little Leon might be ready for round two.

Then she had started mouthing off about how useless he was and how he should get another job and pretty much the same nonsense, she was always shoveling at him. He had ignored her for the most part, as he usually did until she said something, which suddenly changed everything.

"And you have the nerve to call that lovin'?" she complained, "That was pitiful! You are one of the most pathetic excuses for a lover I've ever known."

This got his attention. He said, "Jolene, you're only twenty-one years old and we've been together for the past three years. You can't have had all that much experience before me. You don't know what the Hell you're talking about. So why not just shut your stupid mouth and quit while you're ahead."

This angered Jolene and pushed her further, "I've had a lot more experience than you know, Leon," she replied snidely, "In fact . . ." she hesitated for a moment looking at him unsure whether or not to proceed. Then her anger won over and she proclaimed, "Just last week your so-called best friend Kyle gave me the most incredible ride of my life!"

This stopped Leon in his tracks. What had she just said? Kyle? Kyle had been his best friend since childhood, and he often thought Jolene was simply jealous of their friendship. Jolene saw she had struck a nerve maybe even done some major damage so she continued her assault, "Yeah, that's right, Leon. Me and Kyle humping and sweating like a couple of rutting animals. How do you like that news, Quick-draw McGraw?"

"Was she serious?" he thought. Her and Kyle behind his back? At first, he was sure she was just making it all up to get to him, but seeing the look on her face; he began to believe it just might be true. How could she have done this? And how could Kyle have done this? She surely must had wanted to hurt him badly and Lord knew she had just done it but why now; and why with Kyle?

He imagined her and Kyle sitting in bed, Kyle drinking Leon's beer, smoking Leon's dope and laughing at Leon behind his back. They were living it up on his dime enjoying making a fool of him, and no one made a fool of Leon Trakowsky.

Jolene wasn't very bright and didn't seem to know when to quit, "And I'll tell you something else, Leon . . ." she persisted in her taunting. "Kyle is an amazing lover. We've been doing it regularly for the past four months. Yeah that's right, big man. I've been banging him like crazy behind your back, and you didn't even know about it. That's just how stupid you are. We did it right there in the bed you and me just left. Truth is, we did it in every room of this piece of crap apartment including right there on the kitchen table where you're sitting right now. And you know what? I'll bet Kyle will even be willing and able to give me the baby I want, if he hasn't already."

This was more than Leon could handle. His fury overtook him, and he backhanded her across the face spinning her in the air knocking glasses, plates and food from the table. She fell and slammed her head against the corner of the table on her way down ending up lying motionless on the kitchen floor.

He recalled bending down checking to see if she was breathing calling her name and slapping her gently on the face to see if she would respond, but she didn't. Then he saw the blood pool below her head forming a puddle on the dingy linoleum and he knew he was in a world of trouble. Was she dead? Had he killed her?

After a few moments, her eyes flicked, slowly opening. She reached her hand up to her head and felt the blood. She looked at Leon with fury and in a disoriented voice said, "You're in big trouble now mister. I'm calling the cops and you're going to jail."

She slowly tried to get up but was weak and couldn't quite manage it. Leon tried to reason with her, "Jolene listen. It was an accident. I didn't mean it. You hit your head. I'll call for help. Just don't say anything about this to the cops. Please."

Her face clouded with anger, "We're done Leon. We're quits! I've had it with you."

Then rage overtook him like a blood red cloak as he blacked out. When he came to his hands were around Jolene's throat, and she lay dead on the floor her lips turning blue and her eyes bulging out of her head looking up at him with a filmy death stare. What had he done? He had to get away to think and to figure out what he should do next.

So there he was driving down a road to who-knows-where with absolutely no idea what his next move should be. He was relatively sure no one had seen him leave that night though he knew his fingerprints would be all over the place including Jolene's throat. Why didn't he take the time to clean up a bit? He had been so confused at the time he had just run.

Skynyrd's *That Smell* continued to blare from his dashboard. Leon slammed his hand against the off button sending the car in to absolute silence.

Up ahead he saw what he was looking for, the left turn that would take him on Center Road through the farmland and small woods of Deer Gap. He slowed down slightly made the turn with a squeal and was on his way. A light rain had started falling again so Leon put on his wipers and put up his windows.

He came to a sharp left curve in the road with no visibility beyond. He should have slowed, but with all of his distractions, he wasn't paying attention to his driving.

As he swerved around the turn, he saw something, which shocked him back to reality. A small herd of four deer stood in the middle of the road directly in his path. He stomped on his break without thinking, and the Firebird went into a skid sliding sideways directly toward the deer. Somehow, miraculously the car stopped just a foot or two from the closest deer ending up sideways across both lanes.

"Jesus, Mary and Joseph H. Christ!" Leon shouted aloud as he sat in shock grasping the steering wheel trying to determine if he was alive or dead. His breathing was rapid, and his hands were shaking and he was sweating profusely. When he began to calm down somewhat, he slowly turned his head to the right to see if he had hit any of the deer. He hadn't felt any impact but assumed whether he had hit one or not the rest would have likely scattered back into the woods. Surely, he couldn't have been lucky enough not to have at least hit one of them. Leon hated deer and the problems they constantly caused for Pennsylvania drivers, often referring to them as "rats with antlers." And the last thing he needed on this night of all nights was to have his car rendered un-drivable by the stupid beasts.

To his surprise, he saw the lead deer a huge buck whose chest was visible through the side window standing calmly next to his car. This was unbelievable! It was acting as still as if Leon hadn't just almost wiped out the entire herd. The buck walked calmly toward the front right front side of the car where it stood staring in through the windshield at Leon motionless. It was a massive beast with a rack of at least twelve points or more.

Where the buck had originally stood, Leon saw three large doe standing likewise appearing without concern. They all seemed to be staring at him and not just looking curiously but looking at him like they knew him. And what was worse, he had a sudden knowing feeling somehow these creatures were aware of what he had done to Jolene that night. He had never had much close contact with wild animals, but he was certain the stares he was getting were in no way normal. Maybe it was just him. Maybe he simply had the heebie-jeebies. Maybe he was getting a case of guilty conscience. Somehow, he knew in his gut, something was very wrong.

Then without warning, the herd started to move as one as if someone suddenly flipped a switch putting into play some sort of choreographed production. As they maneuvered around the car, Leon thought they resembled an animatronics display like he saw once on TV. He didn't understand why the deer hadn't scattered and run back into the woods. He was sure now; however, they would simply walk past his car and be on their way. But this was not to be the case.

The large buck took a position directly in front of Leon's car while two of the doe found their way around the car. One positioned herself next to the driver's side door while one went directly behind the car. The remaining doe stayed positioned right next to his passenger door.

This was getting really, really, strange. What were these stupid animals doing? Leon felt his gut tighten as it often did when he sensed danger.

As if on command all four of the deer simultaneously raised up on their hind legs letting their forelegs drop onto the car with incredible thunderous bang. The sound inside of the car was deafening as Leon threw his hands up to his ears too late to stop the noise. The impact felt like it would rattle the fillings from his teeth.

The buck in the front of the car had caved in the hood of the Firebird causing steam to rise from underneath. This steam came up against the buck's side singeing its fur and turning its flesh pink causing sever blistering, yet the buck didn't flinch or pull away. It continued to apply pressure to the hood crushing it further, all the while being burned by the steam yet never taking its piercing black eyes off Leon.

The doe behind the car had crushed the trunk area. Both of the doe on opposing sides of the car had brought their forelegs down hard on the roof of the car smashing it downward toward Leon's head. He instinctively had ducked down low in the driver's seat, and now he was hunkered below the steering column.

The force of the smashed roof caused both side windows to break as the safety glass crushed into a spider web of cracks before sagging down outside the doors and falling to the ground. The doe on each side of the car continued to close in tighter pressing their bodies snugly against the sides of the car their stomachs filling the void previously occupied by the side windows.

Leon could smell the musky feral sent of these wild beasts. He saw ticks attached to the doe's flesh and insects crawling among the doe's fur. Small gnats swarmed around his face. Looking at both windows, he could see the doe had him trapped inside the vehicle. He tried to restart his engine only to discover it wouldn't turn over obviously the tremendous crushing force of the huge buck straddling the hood had damaged it too severely.

In his rearview mirror Leon could see the doe at the rear of the car was continuing to apply pressure to the trunk lid caving it in further all the while it too was staring at him through the rear window in some sort of trance.

Looking up and out the front windshield as best as he could, Leon saw something appearing from the woods behind the huge buck, but he couldn't make out exactly what it was. It seemed to be some sort of white ethereal shape glowing and floating a few inches above the ground.

As the thing got closer, Leon could see it appeared to be a girl in a white dress with long flowing blonde hair. He couldn't help but look closer at the dress, which was almost transparent allowing a clear view of the girl's body naked beneath. Then he saw something, which made his blood run cold.

As the glowing lady of the woods floated closer, he saw she wasn't some mythical woodland creature. This being, incredibly was Jolene, the same Jolene he had murdered less than an hour earlier.

Impossible, unimaginable but still there she was standing right in front of his car next to the giant buck and dressed in the same white night gown she wore when he had choked the life out of her. How could this possibly be? He looked closer and saw the red marks and deep purple bruises from his strangling hands still visible around her neck. Although resistant to do so, he looked into her face and was shocked to see the bug-eyed death stare still affixed to her face. Her mouth hung agape as a steady stream of crimson drool trickled down her chin. Those milky white film covered eyes were staring at him; staring through him.

The Jolene specter raised her right hand pointing it directly at him and shouted with a mournful moan, "Leeeeoooonnn!"

Panic filled Leon as his instinct for survival kicked in. He started to punch weakly at the stomach of the doe on the driver's side hoping to cause the beast sufficient pain so it would retreat long enough for him to climb out of the car and run, but the creature wouldn't release its grip. In fact, it appeared its stomach was swelling out toward Leon, completely sealing the window frame like some type of freakish balloon. Leon looked across to the right and saw the other doe's stomach swelling in a similar manner as well. Behind him, the doe at the rear of the car had climbed up further onto the trunk spreading its front legs as far as it could, hugging the back window. All around the car the wind was blowing as leaves and twigs flew through the air.

The buck on the front of the car had also slid up higher onto the hood its enormous snout now just inches from the

windshield and its forelegs likewise spread widely. The
beast snorted as the windshield steamed with two huge
rings from its flaring nostrils. Leon ventured a glance at
the spectral Jolene thing seeing her lips were moving
uttering some sort of silent incantation. She now held a
long stick in her hand waving it like a wand. Forest dirt
and debris swirled around her in a steady upward stream
and it looked like she were standing in the eye of a small
hurricane.

Again, in a synchronized performance, the deer all
started to simultaneously spasm with tremors. The car
shook manically with the tremendous force of the quaking
beasts.

Leon heard what sounded like a slight tearing in his left
ear and noticed a small hole was opening in the stomach of
the doe blocking his driver's side window. A thin stream of
blood trickled from the opening as a tiny tendril like finger
of pink flesh worked its way out of the hole steadily
enlarging the opening. Leon looked at the doe on the right
and saw something similar happening. The inside of the
car filled with an indescribable odor so fowl Leon couldn't
help but vomit onto the passenger seat adding more
noxious smells to the already unbearable stench.

Looking back at the doe on the passenger side Leon
saw the organ poking its way free of the doe's stomach was
a six inch long flapping section of intestine spraying blood
and stomach contents all around the inside of the car. Bile
and blood splattered against his face. His screams of terror
resulted in the foul contents flying into his mouth. He spat
repeatedly between his cries in an attempt to relieve
himself of the disgusting discharge.

Somehow, these creatures' intestines were crawling
impossibly out of their abdomens, snaking their way
toward him. He put up his hands to protect his face, but
the winding intestines coming from both sides of the car
wrapped themselves around his wrists pulling them back
until he was sitting low in the driver's seat facing forward,
his arms splayed outward leaving him trapped against the
seat unable to move. His left arm was tight against the
chest of the doe on the driver's side, and he could feel the
steady beat of the beast's heart against his arm.

Leon tried to get his legs up to kick at the windshield but found them trapped under the steering wheel. At the front of the car the Jolene apparition continued chanting her spells amid the swirling vortex of forest debris as the buck crawled ever closer up the front of the car. The Jolene vision seemed to swirl slowly and float upward in the vortex then settle down again repeating this impossible floating and settling over and over.

The buck forced itself up on its front legs while the doe all hugged the car quaking and twitching uncontrollably. The buck lifted its massive head then crashed its mighty rack down into the windshield smashing through the glass, stippling Leon's face with shards of glass as the sharp tips of the antlers stopped just inches from his face, which was bleeding from what seemed like hundreds of small cuts.

The huge buck was still alive thrashing back and forth, trying to gore Leon. Its pointed antlers were slashing frighteningly close to his face. In its savage attack, the buck had suffered a major cut to its throat flooding its hot blood down onto Leon's jeans. He could feel the warmth of the beast's blood as the creature's life drained away. With a spasm and shudder, the buck stopped moving, and Leon knew it was dead. Not that it did him much good as he was still held immobile by the intestine ropes of the two doe.

Then, without warning, both of the snaking intestines released their grips of Leon's wrists as the doe on both sides of the car collapsed to the ground dead. Leon strained to look past the buck's head out the shattered front window to see the Jolene creature seemed to be gone now as was the swirling whirlwind of forest debris.

Leon reached down with his left hand releasing the driver's side door, which surprisingly creaked open bringing in blessedly refreshing night air. With all of his strength, Leon reached up grabbed the dead buck's rack and pushed it forward until he was able to turn his head sideways and squirm out of the car. He lay on the ground on his back looking up at the night sky, shocked to be alive.

He wondered how much of what had happened here was real and how much he had imagined. He thought perhaps he had struck his head and all of this was a hallucination. He looked to his left and saw the doe lying dead with its guts spilled out onto the road. He saw the bulk of the enormous buck with its head pushed through the windshield. Perhaps he had crashed into the herd after all, had been rendered unconscious, and then had dreamt the rest especially the part about Jolene. That made a lot more sense; maybe it had all been a bad dream.

He lay back on the chilling ground looking up into the sky taking a deep relieving breath. The trees formed a canopy over the highway with only a few places where he could see the stars peeking through.

Then he heard someone call his name.

"Leeeeooonnn!" the voice moaned. He lifted himself up on one elbow and once again saw the illuminated Jolene vision floating from behind the back of the Firebird. "Why did you kill me, Leon?" the vision asked in its mournful drone.

Leon attempted to sit up to run away, but before he could, the remaining doe ran from behind the back of the Firebird charging him, hooves thrashing. Leon tried desperately to fight off the beast with his fists, but it was useless.

The doe smashed Leon's left forearm crushing the man's wrist and snapping his elbow joint. Leon screamed in pain. The beast rose up on its hind legs a second time and came down on the inner part of Leon's thigh muscle rendering his leg temporarily paralyzed. Again he screamed in agony.

The Jolene specter spoke again, "Leon. You didn't have to kill me. I wasn't serious. I was just playing a game with you. I never messed with Kyle. I was only trying to make you jealous, you know how I do that sometimes. But you had to lose control. You had to kill me. Kill me, and your unborn child. That's right, Leon, your baby."

Leon looked on in amazement the guardian doe standing by waiting for its next orders. "But . . . but you said . . ." he stammered.

"Yes. I said a lot of things most of which weren't true. I was just testing to see if you really loved me, and if you were ready to settle down and raise a family. I guess you weren't ready after all. Were you, Leon? How can a murderer be a husband and a father?"

"But how was I to know?" Leon tried to reason.

The Jolene thing chuckled hideously and began to sing, the words to *That Smell*, as a shudder of cold dread shot down Leon's spine.

She said, "There is a special room in Hell for baby killers like you, Leon. Be sure to think of me from time to time as you suffer countless tortures for all of eternity."

The vision nodded toward the remaining doe, which once again rose up on her hind legs and in just a few moments crushed Leon's skull to a bloody pulp. Soon Leon's head was nothing more than a gelatinous mass dangling from the bloody stump of a neck. The doe stopped its attack walking slowly toward the glowing vision of Jolene. Without a word, the two turned heading back deep into the woods of Deer Gap.

DEVIL'S DEN

It was October 31, Halloween night a cold and gloomy evening perfect for the spirit of the season. It was the time also known as All Hallows Eve. Brian stood outside his garage chilled to the bone but not letting the cold deter his annual vigil because this was his night. This was the night, for which he waited all year the night when he had the opportunity to shine.

Halloween was Brian's favorite holiday so much so every year he transformed his two-car garage into a very special Halloween haunt complete with detailed artistic scenery, props, gags and the occasional animatronics, whenever his budget would permit. Brian put all of his spare time and energy into his special haunt despite the occasional grumblings from his wife. He'd always attempt to explain to her, this was his hobby; it was his stress relief. He'd describe how when compared to other hobbies such as golf or hunting his actual costs in terms of both time and money were still a fraction of what those other hobbies required.

Each year Brian would open up his haunt to the public and allow all the local kids and their parents to rise to the challenge and venture inside enjoying it free of charge. For him, just hearing their compliments about his artwork and craftsmanship was worth much more than any fee he might consider charging. He especially loved when the teenage girls would run from the garage screaming in terror. Then he knew he had done his job correctly.

Another part of this annual ritual was after Halloween was over he'd donate many of his props and scenery to a local not-for-profit haunt and immediately began planning, designing and building for the next Halloween season.

Each year, Brian chose a different theme for his haunt, and as the word spread, it was common for as many as several hundred people to pass through his haunted garage in a single Halloween night. Brian would always push the envelope each year trying to see just how much he could get away with before someone in the neighborhood complained. For example, the theme for this particular season was a depiction of the horrors of Hell.

Brian realized he was going to have to walk a fine line with his theme, as he lived in a very conservative area in Pennsylvania. He knew having a sign displayed at his haunt reading something like "Horrors of Hell" wouldn't go over very well with the locals. Not wanting to upset the neighbors in his subdivision, he reluctantly toned it down a bit and created a large banner to hang outside calling his haunt, "Devil's Den." He knew no matter what degree of unspeakable horrors he depicted inside the garage, as long as the outside was inoffensive, he could get away with almost anything.

As always, the night had been another great success with over two hundred and fifty individuals coming through his haunt. Brian counted each one with a hand counter. Most of the kids dressed in a variety of trendy costumes, and many parents came along acting as chaperons. Some of the parents were dressed in Halloween costumes as well while others opted for street clothes. Some of the less adventurous parents with older children chose to stay out at the main sidewalk allowing their children to experience the haunted garage either alone or with friends. Brian loved how a party atmosphere seemed to take over the entire neighborhood on Halloween night, and he loved that his haunt had a lot to do with keeping the atmosphere going.

Most of the smaller children had long since tuckered out and had quit for the night, many needing to be carried home in their parents' arms exhausted. The only trick-or-treaters remaining for the last half hour or so seemed to be older teenagers.

Brian looked at his watch and saw it was about 8:30. Official trick-or-treating started promptly at 6:00 pm and ended by 9:00 pm. During the earlier years of his haunt, he would often shut everything down by 8:15 or so as the crowd started thinning out, but as the garage's popularity grew so did the crowds, which often stayed past the official end of festivities. One year he had his wife video tape the line of over thirty people waiting to enter his haunt. That line had snaked down the driveway and partway up the sidewalk. This year the cold evening seemed to be taking its toll on the crowd as he was also beginning to get uncomfortably chilled as well. There didn't seem to be another soul in site so he decided perhaps this would be a good time to call it a night.

He walked down to the end of his driveway looking up and down the street checking for any last minute stragglers and latecomers but saw no one in site. He slowly walked back toward his two open garage doors taking a few moments to admire the quality of his workmanship. He had gone to great pains to create a facade resembling a stone wall with red illumination shining outward from inside the garage between cracks in the rocks projecting what he hoped would appear to be an image of the fire and brimstone of Hell. Across the top of the garage hung the "Devil's Den" banner and stealing a line from Dante's Divine Comedy he had a subtext below reading "All hope abandon ye who enter here."

As he reluctantly prepared to close his garage doors for yet another successful Halloween season, he noticed a lone costumed figure shuffling up his driveway heading straight toward his haunt. Brian looked at him with a level of surprise as he had just checked the street not more than what he believed to be a minute ago and saw no one, unless he unknowingly had stood admiring his work for much longer than he originally thought.

"Where did he come from?" Brian wondered to himself.

Brian assumed the kid was most likely an older teenager possibly close to the age where it was past time to stop going out in costume and mooching free candy because the kid stood over six feet tall.

Looking closer at the costume the kid wore Brian realized his parents must have spent a small fortune on the outfit because it was, to say the least, incredibly realistic. Brian considered himself something of an expert in all things horror and Halloween related having been a life-long fan of the genre.

"Unbelievable!" Brian said with genuine appreciation complementing the teen's attire. "That's the most amazing costume I've ever seen." The kid didn't reply but just looked at the scenery with fascination as if he had never seen such a display before.

Brian was enjoying the kid's enthusiasm with his work more than he cared to admit appreciating any teenager who could convince his parents to spend their hard-earned money on such an obviously costly extravagance as the Halloween costume, must be someone who understands the importance of quality artwork. Brian beamed with pride. If pride was truly one of the seven deadly sins then at that moment Brian was one of the biggest sinners in town.

That was the real reason he created this haunt every year: for the sheer pride and adulation he bestowed upon himself when someone such as the teen truly enjoyed his work, his art.

As the boy, at least he assumed it was a boy, stood looking curiously at the scenery; Brian took the opportunity to examine the teen's costume in detail. It portrayed of some sort of huge hulking demon with long shiny muscular arms hanging to the ground ending in large gnarled hands fitted with talon-like claws. The huge rubber feet he wore also appeared to have similar claws. The entire costume seemed to be made of some sort of rubbery or leathery flesh-like material glistening in light from a nearby streetlight.

At first, Brian thought to himself, "Latex. It must be latex." Then he decided that perhaps he might be mistaken, as surely, creating such an incredibly realistic costume from so much latex would be astronomical in cost. Brian couldn't see a single seam, a joint or any suggestion the costume might actually be a costume at all.

This indicated to him some sort of overlay of latex or other makeup had to have been used to disguise the seams.

Again, he thought to himself, "Amazing." He wondered if perhaps this boy's parents might not just be rich but they might somehow be involved in the movie business. Obviously, a professional of some sort was required to create a costume as incredible as this one.

The head of the costume resembled a wild boar with giant tusks protruding up from its lower jaw, a pig-like snout, pointed ears and a mane of long hair flowing back between two ram-like horns jutting from a Neanderthal sloping brow shading two yellow-red eyes. Incredibly, the outfit actually emitted an odor, which smelled sweaty, animal-like and feral. Brian assumed perhaps they might have actually used some less expensive material it after all and this would explain the cause of the foul odor emitting from the outfit. That would have been a good choice however, as it gave the costume a more sinister level of realism, which was frightening and chilling.

"I wish you could have been here earlier," Brian said to the boy by way of a compliment, "That costume would have been perfect for attracting people to my haunted garage especially considering the theme I chose for this year."

"Theme?" the kid questioned in a deeply masculine, raspy, almost growling tone, "What is it you mean by theme?"

Brian thought to himself, "This kid is great. I love it. Just listen to that voice, the way he never breaks character." He decided he'd have to learn more about this kid and maybe get his name and phone number. Anyone who would go to such extremes with such a level of commitment to the holiday had a welcome place in any of Brian's future Halloween activities.

Brian explained, "Every year I choose a particular theme for my Halloween haunt and this year my theme was 'The Horrors of Hell,' so I came up with the name Devil's Den."

"Devil's Den. Horrors of Hell. Interesting," the boy replied still using the gravely deep "monster" voice while studying the sign hanging above the garage.

Brian subtly scrutinized the head of the costume still in awe at the extent the guy went to in creating the disguise.

He must have used Hollywood-quality individual custom fit latex facial appliances because the mask was flawless catching every slight change and nuance of his expressions; it was astounding. Brian suspected to put together a costume of such an incredible quality had to cost over several thousand dollars. Suddenly the few bucks he spent on his entire haunt seemed trivial. This kid was the real deal.

"May I see the inside of your 'Devil's Den?'" the boy inquired snapping Brian out of his deep contemplation.

"Of course." Brian offered. "It would be my pleasure. And when your tour is finished you must tell me more about yourself and for example where you got that fantastic costume." The young man in the demon costume didn't respond.

The two entered the garage through a black curtained doorway, and Brian proceeded to show him each one of the props he had designed and artistically created himself specifically for the haunt. He had mannequins dressed in tattered clothing suspended with wires, which were supposedly piercing their flesh. He had another section where he depicted individuals being tortured by a variety of sadistic methods, one more horrible than the next. He had one body whose limbs were in the process of being ripped off by small, animated demons about two feet tall. He had another whose intestines were slowly being removed from a person by a winding type of mechanism controlled by yet another demon. Brian had seen this type of torture in a book about actual torture techniques practiced during the middle ages. There was a good deal of fake blood, smoke billowing from strategically disguised fog machines and a sound track of painful screaming to add an air realism to the show.

The boy in the costume stared at all of the activities seemingly captivated by what he saw, "Where did you get your ideas?" he asked. "What was your inspiration for such an interesting scene?"

This was exactly the kind of inquiry Brian loved hearing every Halloween season and he took great pleasure in telling anyone who would listen all about his creative process how he painstakingly worked for realism and details about how each prop was made. People who knew Brian said he was the type of person who you could ask for the time and he'd tell you how to build a clock.

"Well," Brian said, "most of what you see here I usually just make up. You know I use my imagination and think about what Hell would really be like. You know? Would it be fire and brimstone or would it just be a dark nothingness? Would it be filled with little gremlin-like demons like I have depicted here? Or would it be controlled by huge hulking creatures, similar to, well similar to your costume?"

"Interesting," the boy repeated. "That's quite an imagination you have there."

Brian continued, "Well, thanks for the compliment, but it's not just my imagination. You see there is plenty of information on the Internet about different depictions of Hell throughout the ages, so there is a wealth of information available. And as long as I can come up with some frightening images of what Hell might look like, that is to say, if Hell really existed then I have done my work properly."

The kid stopped for a moment turning slowly to look directly at Brian, "Did you just say if Hell actually existed?"

"Excuse me?" Brian asked.

"I believe you said, 'If Hell actually existed,'" the demonic looking character repeated. "I assume you mean to imply Hell doesn't exist for real."

"Yes, of course," Brian replied. "That's exactly what I meant. Everyone knows Hell is no more real than Santa Clause or the Easter Bunny. We all understand Hell was just a concept devised by the wealthy ruling classes back in the old days to keep their peasants in line. Those sad people were poor beyond comprehension and just ripe for revolution. Only the fear of condemnation to a horrible fictitious place such as Hell provided by the church which, by the way was run by the rich, was successful in keeping the peasants in their place."

"So, what you're saying Hell is a lie nothing more than a fictional concept?" the teen inquired. Brian was surprised at the level of maturity from the boy, having the courage to discuss such a highly intellectual concept with an adult.

Brian replied with some degree of impatience, "Yes, that's exactly what I'm saying. Of course, Hell doesn't exist. And that's that."

"So then you believe there's no Heaven either?" he inquired.

"Not like it's any of your business," Brian said suddenly taking a defensive posture, "but, of course, I believe in Heaven! But not in Hell."

"That seems a bit odd for you to take such a rigid and unusual position," the costumed boy interjected. "If you took the time to look around, you'd find everything in the universe has its opposite. You know the idea, 'for every action there is an equal and opposite reaction.' Or perhaps Yin and Yang and so forth might be more to your understanding."

The kid was really starting to get on Brian's nerves as he was already cold and tired and had just about enough of Halloween, not to mention enough of this kid for this year. He decided he wouldn't be asking this smart Alec back next year or at any time in the future; he was simply too annoying.

"Look, kid," Brian said finally, "I'd love to sit and argue theology with you some other time, but right now it is cold and I'm tired and ready to call it a night. I no longer care who you are or how much money your old man spent on your fancy costume so let's just end this discussion like this. I believe there is no Hell, there never was a Hell and there never will be a Hell. And there's nothing you or anyone else in the universe can do or say to convince me otherwise."

"I beg to differ," the costumed young man replied. Then he did a very strange thing. He lifted his long right arm and started twirling his gnarled index finger in the air in a counter-clockwise motion, the yellowed fingernail of the costumed hand glistening. Again, despite his frustration, Brian couldn't help but be astonished by how realistic looking the kid's disguise was; the long hideous fingers looking as if they were actual living appendages.

Suddenly Brian heard a ripping sound from his left and looked over to see a large tear about six feet long and a few inches wide opening unbelievably in the middle of the air.

He was shocked by the sudden appearance of what seemed to be some sort of long thin portal hanging suspended in the air before him, its middle about a foot wide tapering off to nothing at the top and the bottom. From deep inside the opening, a foul, sulfur-like odor poured out, and Brian noticed how the edges of the opening were glowing with a white-hot fire.

From inside the gash long snake-like tendrils emerged dancing through the air in a serpentine fashion. At the ends of the tendrils, tiny human-like hands appeared, each with long sharp looking talons. The tendrils rushed out grabbing hold of Brian's ankles, pulling him quickly off his feet and slamming his back on the hard concrete garage floor. Brian screamed in agony as he felt the incredible heat from the slimy tendril things melting the very flesh off his legs and dissolving the meat into a bubbling steaming soup right down to the bone. Then the hands gripped tightly on the remaining anklebones slowly hauling him forward.

Brian looked up at the horrid creature realizing the thing, the hideous monstrosity hovering over him, was no teenager in an overpriced Halloween costume; somehow, incredibly, it was some sort of real demon. That meant Hell and the tortures it had to offer must be just as real. Brian understood what a complete fool he had been. An expression flashed into his mind amid all the pain he was suffering; "Give the Devil his due".

"Consider this a research project for you, Brian, old boy," the demonic thing said. "You are going to get to see firsthand what Hell is really like. Unfortunately you won't be able to bring the knowledge back with you since you'll never be coming back."

As the tendrils pulled Brian into the opening, the hot edges flayed the flesh away from his body. He screamed with incredible agony the likes of which he had never imagined. Yet his cries for help simply blended in with the sound track, which had been playing his garage all night long.

Hundreds of small spider-like creatures crawled out of the opening walking up his burning legs. Brian saw in horror the things had tiny human faces with blazing red eyes staring at him with fury. They opened their tiny mouths, and he saw each on held a mouth-full of needle-like teeth. Immediately the spider things began devouring him alive. Brian's screaming continued, unnoticed.

"By the way, Brian," the demon chided, "I should mention not only is Hell real, but it's eternal and you'll get to suffer and die in ways much worse than this over and over again for all of eternity. But you should enjoy yourself; it's like having Halloween, every day of your life."

When Brian was finally pulled completely into the abyss the creature stretched the opening and climbed inside turning to take one last look at the haunt, shaking its head and uttering a sinister chuckle.

THE HOUSE ON THE HILL

The dilapidated old house stood high atop the Market Street hill overlooking the lower half of the town of Ashton like some sort of hideous monument to a time long since forgotten in Schuylkill County, Pennsylvania.

Every kid in town believed the place was cursed or haunted or both though the presumption could never be verified. There were so many stories and legends surrounding the house it was hard to distinguish between what was real, what was imagined and what was completely fabricated.

For example, one tale told of a pair of reclusive elderly sisters who lived in the house during the 1920's and who locals believed to be witches. Many neighbors during that time complained their dogs and cats had gone missing, certain the two strange siblings had taken them. Perhaps the witches used them in some bizarre satanic ritual then boiled them in a stew pot for dinner. The legend claimed because of the sisters' satanic involvement, their souls were doomed to roam the halls of the house for as long as it existed.

Another story dating back to the 1930s told of a husband who had returned to the house early from work one day catching his wife in the act with a former friend of his. In a fit of jealous rage, the husband grabbed a machete from the nearby closet, killed them both and then decapitated them. Next, having gone irrevocably insane, he skewered their heads on the ends of long wooden poles, which he hung out the third floor window for all of the townspeople to see. The story said shortly thereafter, he used the same blade to slit his own throat just before jumping headfirst from the roof of the building and smashing to the pavement below in a heap of broken bones. Legend said the lovers' decapitated ghosts still wondered from room to room trying to find their missing heads.

The last owner of the house was a seventy-five year old racketeer named Lamar "Bishop" Milner. He was a well-known local king pin believed to be involved in most of the shady activities in the county; gambling, robbery, burglary, fencing stolen goods, whatever. One night while the old man slept two thugs broke into the house and beat Milner with clubs crushing his skull leaving him to die in a pool of bloody brain matter. They supposedly dragged a safe from the building and forced it open a few miles out of town. Rumor had it Milner may have hidden thousands of dollars inside the house and the money was still there just waiting to be discovered. There were also stories about missing local gangsters who, through the years, had run afoul of Bishop and were rumored to have been killed and buried in the basement of the house.

The stories surrounding the house on the hill were as numerous and varied as the people who told them. Whether actually haunted or not, the place had been abandoned since the late 1950's and now stood in ruins a hollow shell of what it once was. Most of the glass had been broken out of the windows by vandals; its shutters hung askew. The roof of the house had stopped doing its job many years ago so the snow and rain was free to leak inside rotting the supportive wood structure. For the past ten years signs reading, "condemned," "danger – do not enter" and "no trespassing" hung on all of the doors and access areas in an attempt to keep young daring teens from entering the building. For the most part, these were unnecessary as most locals stayed as far away from the deteriorating structure as possible. The building would have been torn down years earlier but for some political or legal snafu which was holding up the demolition.

Down the hill from the house, a crowd of young boys was gathered apparently involved in a serious discussion.

"I'm gonna do it," fourteen-year-old Neil Simpson said to the crowd of boys all of whom were staring at him with an assortment of looks ranging from awe to incredulous.

Several of them shook their heads in disbelief, knowing no one had ever considered doing such a thing.

Then Neil asked, "Who's going to go in with me?" Each of the kids in the group looked at each other as if Neil had just asked them if they could sprout wings and fly. Not a single one of them would ever agree to an idea like that.

"You're crazy, Neil," one of the boys said pointing up to the top of the hill at the dismal structure. "There's no way you would ever get any of us to go in there with you!"

"Come on, Carl. You don't really believe place is haunted do you?" Neil asked. "It's 1969 for Christ's sake, not 1669. How can you believe that crap?" Neil was addressing his best friend and classmate, Carl Blaker.

Carl replied, "It doesn't matter what I believe or don't believe. I ain't goin' anywhere near the inside of that place. For starters, it's not safe."

Neil looked at the rest of the gathering of neighborhood kids most of them younger than he and Carl some as young as six years old. "Ain't any of you got the guts to come with me? Or are all of you just a bunch of pussies?" None of the boys replied they all looked at the ground or at each other not willing to meet his gaze.

"No problemo, el pussios," he said in his best pseudo-Spanish impression. "I'll do it all by my lonesome. And after tonight, you can all line up to smooch my lily white butt because I'll be the king of the neighborhood."

The boys all looked at each other with astonishment. Neil was really going to do the unthinkable; he was going to walk through the awful house on the hill at night.

Neil had gotten the wild idea from watching a rerun on TV of a 1959 Vincent Price movie called "House On Haunted Hill." Price's character was an eccentric old guy who invited five strangers to spend the night in his haunted house. It was, in his opinion, cheesy and not very scary, but it did give him the inspiration for doing something cool with Ashton's own supposedly haunted house. He came up with the idea to get a few kids to walk through the place at night then find some type of keepsake and bring it out to show the rest of the neighborhood gang. He even figured if the item they found was cool enough they might display it in their tree shack.

However, not everyone thought the idea was quite as cool as Neil did and as a result, he found himself in an awkward situation. If he backed out now, it would look like he was a coward and afraid to act on his own idea. But if he went in that God-forsaken house, he might have to do so alone. Although the idea terrified him, he had to keep up his false-bravado and what was much worse he actually had to go through with it.

Dusk seemed to arrive much too quickly as the sun set like a glowing red fire ball against the distant horizon. The group of young boys had met at eight o'clock as darkness approached and had all huddled together standing as far away from the house as was possible. They were there to verify Neil did what he said he was going to do, but they didn't plan to get any closer to the foreboding structure than was necessary.

"Last chance," Neil chided sounding much more confident than he actually was, "Last chance to step up to the plate and be a real man."

The group looked among each other to see if anyone would take the challenge but none did. Neil said, "Fine. Suit yourselves. I'll be back to see you losers in a few minutes."

"Neil. Maybe you shouldn't do it," Carl said in an attempt to get his friend to back out of the potentially dangerous situation. "It just ain't safe in there. The place is falling down. You could get hurt or killed. And if you changed your mind, we'd be cool about it. Nobody would call you a chicken or nothing. Would we, boys?"

All of the boys shook their heads. There was no way any of them would risk having Neil think they would call him a chicken; he would likely pound them senseless for sure. Besides, none of them really wanted him to go into the house and risk injury or death.

Neil offered a mock salute to the boys saying, "See you boys, I'll be back with a trophy from the haunted house on the hill. That is unless I find some of Bishop Milner's cashola. 'Cause if I do then I'll be too busy counting money to come out." Then he laughed.

Looking uncertain, the boys seemed to be reconsidering their original reluctance to go along. They had all heard the stories about Milner and believed there might actually be a stash of money somewhere in the house. Then looking up at the hulking building in the eerie light from the rising moon, they decided they wouldn't change their minds for all the money in the world.

Standing silently, the boys watched as Neil turned on his flashlight and adjusted his empty backpack. He figured it might be a good idea to have the pack in case he found several valuables or perhaps a stack of money.

Neil took several tentative steps up the front stairs of the house being careful to avoid areas where the boards had rotted away. He looked back every few steps as if he were contemplating changing his mind but reluctantly went on.

As he approached the front door, Neil hoped he might find it locked and wouldn't be able to get inside giving him an easy out. After all, the place was condemned and trespassing was prohibited, so it seemed logical the door might be locked. But, to his unpleasant surprise, the door opened freely. He noticed the front window was also missing so he supposed there was little reason to lock the front door anyway.

With one last look back, Neil pushed open the door and entered the house. He planned to leave the front door open for an easy get away, but as he passed into the front room, the door slammed shut behind him with a crash. Broken remnants of window glass flew onto the front porch.

Outside the sound of the slamming door caused the startled group of boys to jump as one. Two of the youngest boys turned and ran down the steep hill, heading home for the night already more frightened than they wanted to be.

Carl stood at the head of the group of four remaining boys shaken but not ready to run just yet. Reaching into his front pocket his hand found his father's old aluminum cased cigarette lighter. He hadn't known what prompted him to bring the lighter with him, but he had a feeling it might come in handy.

The evening had become very quiet the cool air barely moving. Carl wasn't paying attention to the other boys who were murmuring nervously among themselves. He was too busy focusing on the front door of the house almost as if willing the door to open and for Neil to come walking out flashing his stupid grin.

Suddenly the all heard a horrifying scream coming from inside the house, a scream Carl immediately recognized as having come from Neil. Then from behind him Carl heard a series of frightened cries followed by the slapping of PF Flyers against asphalt as the silhouettes of the remaining boys could be seen running away down the hill.

With his heart thumping madly in his chest, Carl stood transfixed unable to move. His initial instinct was to turn and flee, but his best friend was in that horrible house and perhaps hurt. Then he heard another mournful cry coming from inside the house, and without hesitation, he found himself on the front porch with his hand turning the doorknob; stepping onto blackness. Pulling out his dad's lighter and flicking it to life, he was amazed by the amount of light the small device provided.

The first thing Carl noticed about the place was the incredibly musty odor of decay the old house had; the stench was breathtaking. He took a few careful steps forward brushing spider webs out of his way and testing the floorboards for strength. He looked around the front room, which was for the most part empty except for a tattered oval area rug on the floor and a broken mirror hanging on the wall to his left. The wall led to a set of stairs obviously went to the second floor and next to them was an open doorway. As Carl passed the cracked mirror, he thought he caught of glimpse of someone in the mirror watching him. When he turned to look he saw no one. Glancing back at the mirror he saw only his own wide terrified eyes gazing back at him.

The doorway led to a long narrow hall with another doorway branching off to the right just a few feet ahead. As he stepped into the hallway, a large rat ran from the darkness and skittered across his shoe. Carl held back a girlish squeal of fright but accidentally snapped back the lid of the lighter plunging him again into darkness. Before he could reignite the lighter, he was blinded by a flash of bright light from down the hallway coming from the adjacent room. He lifted his arms to shield his eyes and couldn't believe what he saw.

"Carl. Man, oh man! I knew I could count on you," Neil said as he stood holding his flashlight shining it into Carl's now angry eyes.

In his fury Carl shouted, "Simpson, you're a dickhead! We thought you were hurt, man. It sounded like you were being murdered for God's sake!"

"Oh, you mean this," Neil said, letting out another mournful howl. Then he laughed loudly saying, "I'll bet the other kids went running home."

Carl said with a little less anger, "I'll say. I'll bet at least one of them pissed his pants over it." Then both boys broke into a fit of roaring laughter at the thought.

Carl gave an uncomfortable sigh and asked, "So what did you find? You know, for a souvenir."

"Nothing yet," Neil replied with some disappointment. "I haven't had any luck so far. This place seems to be picked clean."

"Well, then. I think we should just grab something, anything and get the heck out of this dump!" Carl said. "This place gives me the creeps. Hey, what's in the room behind you?"

Carl pointed to an old chest of drawers with all the drawers pulled out and smashed to pieces. "Why not just take one of those drawer handles? That might be good enough."

"You gotta be kidding!" Neil argued, "That's just plain idiotic. I can't walk out of here with a stupid drawer handle."

Then something caught Neil's eye. He noticed a glimmer of light reflecting off something across the room. Neil shone his flashlight onto a door on the far wall. "Wow! Now that's really cool!"

The two boys approached the door to examine Neil's discovery; a beautiful cut crystal doorknob.

"Man!" Neil said, "I haven't seen one of these things in a long time. My old man used to have a few of them but sold them because they were worth some major money. Let's snag this one; it will make a great souvenir!"

Before Carl had a chance to consider the idea, Neil reached out and grabbed the glass knob turning it to the right. The door slowly swung toward him, and the boys could see nothing but blackness beyond.

"Cool!" Neil shouted. "I'll bet this leads down to the cellar. These old places always had dirt cellars, and I'll bet that old fart Milner buried his money in the cellar."

Carl replied, "I don't know, Neil. I think we should just get out of here before something bad happens. I don't have a good feeling about this place."

Neil ignored his concern and started walking down the stairs. Carl put his lighter back into his pocket and followed Neil's flashlight beam down the rickety wooden stairway into the basement. When they were about half way down the stairs unknown to them, what they had seen as a beautiful crystal doorknob had reverted to its true form; a rusted, pitted hideous metal knob as the cellar door slammed shut behind them.

"Neil. This is a really bad idea. Let's get out of here," Carl pleaded. But Neil would have no part of it. He was determined to find something of value and his instincts told him the cellar was the place to find it.

"Don't be such a pussy," Neil said. "Just a few minutes longer and if we don't find anything we will go back take the glass door knob and leave. Alright?"

"Alright," Carl said with a disapproving tone, "but just a few more minutes."

"Look. Over there!" Neil said as he pointed his flashlight at the dirt floor about ten feet away from where they stood. Something shiny and metallic was jutting up out of the soil. "It looks like some kind of box."

Neil raced over to the object and started digging the loose dirt with one hand from around the box trying to free it further. He said with excitement, "Here, Carl. Take the flashlight at shine it over here. It looks like some kind of metal lock box or something. I'll bet it's full of dough!"

Carl held the light on the area where Neil was now digging furiously with both hands. He was surprised to see the box was in such good condition. He would have assumed it would have been rusted to some degree after being buried in the ground for so many years but it looked like it was made of shiny brand new metal.

Neil managed to unearth the box and laid it down to see if he could open it. To both boys' surprise and disappointment, there was no lock on the box whatsoever, just a simple flip latch. "Crap!" Neil said. "It ain't locked. That means their probably ain't anything of any value in here or if there was it is probably long gone. Well let's look anyway."

Neil flipped the latch on the lock box and lifted the lid. The boys stood in shock as they stared at a severed human hand. "Jesus!" Neil screamed dropping the box and falling backward onto his butt in front of it. Carl stood staring at the dismembered appendage the flashlight trembling in his hand.

Then the flesh on the hand began to turn from a normal shade of pink to a mottled gray then to a blackish greenish color as the skin bubbled then burst open revealing the white bone below. Maggots crawled about the hand as the foul stench of decomposition began to fill the air. The shiny metallic box transformed before their eyes into a brown, rusted container riddled with holes out of which more maggots crawled.

As Neil stared in astonishment, several long, bony fingers began to rise up from the ground on both sides of his legs. Neither boy saw them as the two were focusing on the horrible appendage in the rusted box. The skeletal hands with only fragments of rotting flesh remaining quickly wrapped around Neil's ankles pulling him down into the sandy soil. Before he realized what was happening, his legs were in the ground up to his knees resembling someone sinking in quick sand.

"Help! Oh my God! No! Help me! Help me, Carl!" he cried in terror.

Carl was bending over shining the flashlight into the box when he heard Neil screaming. He immediately dropped the flashlight to the ground and hooked his forearms under Neil's armpits trying to pull him out. Neil's backpack jammed against his chest hindering his rescue efforts. He was unaware of what was causing Neil to sink into the ground, but he knew he had to help his friend. Tugging with all of his might, Carl managed to pull Neil a few inches backward when he saw reflected in the light of the dropped flashlight a skull-like face rising along with Neil from the earth. Covered with grime, bits of its decomposing flesh dropped from the skull thing onto Neil's legs. One of its eye sockets was empty while from the other a filmy dead eye dangled from a few remaining muscles. Its mouth opened and closed as if trying to say something but no words were spoken. The boys could hear the clacking of its teeth together like a bizarre version of the clattering teeth gag Carl had seen in a joke store, but this was no joke.

Carl pulled with every ounce of strength he could muster but wasn't able to free Neil any further. Neil was crying and screaming at the top of his lungs, and Carl realized he too was screaming just as loudly. Then he felt it. Something took hold of his ankles.

Looking down he saw two more skeletal hands had worked their way out of the ground wrapping themselves around his ankles trying to pull him downward. Letting go of Neil, he fell to the ground on his backside and tried to kick himself free but to no avail; the boney fingers just grabbed him tighter. Then he saw a white curved object arising from the soil in front of eventually becoming another skull with only its empty eye sockets showing at ground level.

Carl suddenly remembered his Dad's cigarette lighter. He reached down into this pocket to retrieve it. He had no idea if it would help or not, but after a few attempts, the flame came to life. Carl pressed the flame against his ankle and the skeletal fingers immediately disintegrated into a cloud of dust settling back down onto the soil. The other griping hand and the skull rising from the dirt were also gone; having returned to dust as well.

Turning quickly Carl brought the lighter around to free Neil only to see the boy was in the dirt over his nose, with only his horrified tear-filled eyes exposed. Before Carl could do anything, his friend went completely under the ground.

"Neil!" the boy screamed in anguish, but his friend was gone.

Where Neil had once been, Carl saw several new boney fingers beginning to emerge from the soil. He quickly got to his feet and grabbing the flashlight ran up the basement steps taking them two at a time, dropping his father's lighter along the way. The lighter landed in a pile of old rags under the steps and immediately caught fire, but Carl didn't realize this as he broke through the door into the side room then ran out into the hall. As he turned left to head for the front door, he heard a high-pitched raspy voice.

"Boy!" the voice called, "Come here, boy. We want to speak with you."

Without thinking, Carl turned and looked down the hall to his right and saw gray glowing images of two very old women, which seemed to float though the air toward him. They were hideous old crones with long boney fingers beckoning him. Immediately he recalled the story of the two witch sisters and turned heading for the front door.

"Come back, boy!" the witch sisters cackled in unison, their laughter hideous.

Carl pulled on the handle of the front door, but it wouldn't open. He could smell smoke and realized the building was on fire. Behind him, he heard a thumping sound and looked up the stairs to see two headless naked beings one man and one woman clumsily staggering down the steps toward him with their arms outstretched. He turned and started to climb out of the broken window when he felt cold hands grabbing him by his arms and pulling him backward throwing him down on the floor. Carl looked up and saw a stocky old man looking down at him. The old man's skull appeared crushed, as was half of his face. His brain was exposed and bits of a grayish ooze dripped from his skull to the floor. The old man bent over toward Carl and the boy could smell his fowl and rancid breath. Then he saw maggots, crawling from the old man's exposed brain.

"Welcome to my house, boy. Or should I say welcome to our house?" the old specter moaned.

Carl was unable to break free of the thing's grip. He looked up and saw a bright glow from across the room coming from the broken mirror. Neil's face appeared in the glass looking down at Carl. His hands pressed tightly against the inside of the mirror as if he were trying to get free, but his eyes looked dead and expressionless with dark black circles beneath them. The last thing the boy saw as the room around him burst into flames and the floor began to collapse was the old man, the two headless beings and the floating witches swarming around him.

It took just moments for the four-story structure to turn into an enormous flaming pyre visible all over town from its perch high atop the hill. By the time the volunteer fire companies arrived, there was nothing to be done except to keep the flames from spreading to other nearby structures.

Later that evening, the parents of the two boys reported them missing. The neighborhood kids each were questioned and tearfully told the police about Neil going inside the building. Several days later when the smoldering heap had cooled down police conducted an investigation; they found the two boys' charred bodies in the basement of the ruins near a blackened cigarette lighter. The official report cited "death by misadventure" stating the two boys must have gone into the house and had been fooling around with the lighter, accidentally set the building on fire and died in the blaze. However, for the rest of the neighborhood boys such a story would never suffice. They believed the house on the hill was responsible and always would.

RETRIBUTION

Leviticus 24:19-20 (King James Version),
[19] *And if a man cause a blemish in his neighbor; as he hath done, so shall it be done to him;*
[20] *Breach for breach, eye for eye, tooth for tooth: as he hath caused a blemish in a man, so shall it be done to him again.*

"When man no longer respects the laws of civilization nor fears the fires of Hell all that remains is anarchy. "
– Thomas M. Malafarina

Bill Watkins looked the Ashton, Pennsylvania chief squarely in the eye explaining, "What I mean was everyone, you, me; every human on the planet has both the propensity for doing incredible good but also has the ability within them to do unspeakable evil."

"Well, maybe I'm just a small town cop and can't quite get my head around what you're trying to suggest, Bill. I've met a lot of very bad and evil people in my life and many of them don't have an ounce of good in them anywhere."

Watkins continued, "I see what you're saying and perhaps I'm making this whole explanation more complicated than it really needs to be. Let's look at it from the opposite angle. Take me for example. I'm traditionally a non-violent man, a man of peace. I don't own a gun nor have I ever hunted or fished. I have never hurt an animal or another man in my entire life. I'm fifty years old and have never even been in a fistfight. I am by nature an easy going, easy to get along with sort of person. Yet, after what happened last year, I've had many opportunities to look deep into my own soul and what I've seen there frightens me incredibly. I've learned even a person like me has the potential to inflict unspeakable pain on his fellow man under the right, or I should say wrong set of circumstances."

Chief Seiler let out a sigh and said, "I think I understand what you're saying, Bill. However, your situation is extreme. I mean for God's sake Bill, he raped and butchered your wife. And then he suffocated your children in their sleep. I recognize how something like that could cause someone to think incredibly horrible and vengeful thoughts. Hell, if it was me, I might feel like I was going a bit off the deep end myself. But, the bottom line here is no matter what you might say or no matter what you want to believe, the fact is you didn't go crazy. You didn't hurt or kill anyone. You're still the same Bill Watkins you always were. You may have wished harm on that scumbag Wilbur Donovan, but I'd consider such thoughts perfectly normal. I've wished harm on him myself plenty of time during the past year. The thing is, you haven't acted on your thoughts. You're still the same good man you always were, and I respect you for that."

"But don't you see Chief, that's where you're mistaken?" Watkins corrected, "After what I've been through I'll never ever be the same. Yes, I may be trying to live my life as closely to normal as is possible. And maybe I'm finally able to start putting all of this behind me, but I've looked into my inner soul and I've seen a part of myself resembling a creature straight from the bowels of Hell itself and because of that revelation, I'll never be the same. I now know what I'm capable of."

"Alright then, Bill. I can see we're going to have to agree to disagree about this. I'm not as educated a man as you are and perhaps I'll never completely be able to understand what you're suggesting. But just so you know I think you're a better man than me just for surviving all of this the way you did."

"Thanks, Chief. I too have a lot of respect for you and the work you do, so your opinion means a lot to me. But speaking of Donovan, have you located him yet? I have to tell you I'm not comfortable knowing he escaped from jail and is on the loose."

"Well," Seiler said reluctantly, "we haven't found him yet, which is why we have a patrol car stationed outside your house round the clock. We're genuinely concerned he may return for you. This is especially worrisome since you're our key witness, having been tied up and forced to watch the entire horrible crime."

Bill winced visibly then regained his composure and replied, "I know, and I understand your apprehension. What you have to realize is I don't fear this man nor do I fear death any longer. I believe when I die no matter what happens here on Earth, I'll be reunited with my Cindy and the kids once again. If my death is to be attained at the hand of a lunatic like Donovan then so be it. In fact there are times when I think I'd almost welcome it."

"But you see, Bill my job is to keep you safe and alive and to bring Donovan back in to face a jury."

Watkins seemed to contemplate this for a time then asked, "So how was it then Donovan managed to escape custody in the first place?"

Seiler explained with a degree of embarrassment, "It was a very bad situation, Bill. Our local constable was transporting Donovan from the county jail in Yuengsville to the prison up in Franksville when his car with Donovan inside was broadsided by an unidentified black van. The constable was knocked unconscious and when he awoke, Wilbur Donovan and the van were both gone. Obviously, Donovan must have had an accomplice who had some inside information about the transport. We're working 'round the clock to get to the bottom of this. I hope you realize how very sorry we are about this, Bill. I know how it must upset you."

"Initially I have to admit it did, Chief. But I have complete faith in you and your men and I believe within a few days Donovan will either be back in custody or hopefully if he resists arrest he'll end up dead. Either option is fine with me."

"I certainly hope you're right, Bill. And I promise you I'll do everything I can to catch Donovan and to keep you safe in the process."

Watkins stood up indicating it was time for their conversation to end and shook Chief Seiler's hand saying, "Thanks, Chief Seiler. And best of luck. I suspect this will all be over soon."

Seiler felt a strange tingling at the back of his neck. It was the feeling he got when something was a bit off. It was what he called his "cop sense." He was getting a similar vibration from Watkins, which seemed ridiculous. Watkins was the victim in this scenario. Perhaps it was something in Watkins' voice or his body language or perhaps a brief passing look in his eyes. Whatever it was, it made Seiler uneasy. Nonetheless he chose to ignore it and chalk it up to the pressure he was under to apprehend Wilbur Donovan.

"Ah, um, thanks, Bill," Seiler said still a bit uneasily. "You take care and don't worry. We'll have Donovan in a few days, I'm sure."

"I too, am quite certain you will, Chief." Bill Watkins said with a strange smile Seiler hadn't noticed previously. Again, he got the uneasy feeling.

After Seiler left, Watkins closed and relocked his front door. He pulled aside the curtain on the door and observed the patrol car parked on the street in front of his house. He gave a wider version of the same sly and knowing smile Seiler had seen then he turned and headed to the basement, to his special room, to his new hobby, to Mr. Wilbur Donovan.

Watkins had an entire year to prepare for what was to come and took full advantage of the time having constructed a soundproof room in the rear of his basement in an area underground. Although the soil itself probably provided sufficient soundproofing, Bill had taken the extra precaution of studding, insulating and further sealing the room so he felt assured not a single cry or scream would ever escape.

He chuckled at how easy it had been to snatch Donovan from the police and how even now they still had no idea he had been involved. Who would ever suspect peace-loving mild mannered easy-going victimized Bill Watkins? No one would, but then again no one knew of the existence of the new and improved Bill Watkins.

He pulled open the door to the special room and saw Donovan in the dim light of a single bare hanging light bulb looking at Watkins with the most incredible hatred he had ever seen from another human being. He had to laugh to himself knowing soon, that look would be gone forever from the evil man's ruddy face.

Donovan stood strapped and chained naked to a huge rectangular rack made of six-by-six heavy weight pressure treated lumber, the base of which lay cemented twenty-four inches deep into the ground. The rack held him in a vertical position so he'd never have the opportunity to relax. He looked up at Watkins with a crazed stare of hatred, dried blood congealing on his chin. He opened his mouth to scream but all he could manage was a muffled "arragh" sound.

Walking up to an electronic console Watkins powered up a computer. The room was suddenly awash with bright lights as three video cameras came to life. Donovan saw himself displayed from various angles on several large flat screen monitors positioned around the room.

"Just like on the old *I Love Lucy* show," Watkins said smiling, "Did you know Desi Arnez was credited with developing the three camera shoot for situation comedies? Then again I suppose you really don't care very much about things such as that do you?"

"Arrag!" Donovan mumbled from across the room. He struggled against his bonds but soon discovered the effort was futile.

Watkins said, "Mr. Donovan, or can I call you Wilbur? After all, we've been acquainted before. Regardless, welcome to my very special basement entertainment room. I went to great personal expense and risk to bring you here for my amusement. You don't recall what happened to you. Do you? Well, allow me to explain. I was the driver of the black van, which slammed into the constable's car. I was well prepared to kill the man if necessary, but fortunately, I hear he was only slightly injured. I was also lucky you too were knocked unconscious. It saved me the trouble of drugging you. I brought you back here and got you situated in your new, and I should point out, final resting place.

"By the way, feel free to yell and scream to your heart's content. It won't matter since the room is completely sound proof, and as you may have noticed as an extra precaution, I took the liberty of cutting out your filthy rotten tongue. I've already heard enough out of you, and I didn't want your horrific voice spoiling one second of my fun. All I'll need to hear from you from now on are screams of pain.

"You see, Wilbur, not only did you kill my lovely wife and my precious family, but whether you know it or not, you essentially killed me as well. When you bound me and forced me to watch you rape and butcher Cindy, you killed the kind, loving and caring man I once was. In his place, you left a savage creature overflowing with nothing but hatred and a determination to get retribution."

"In fact I just had a conversation on that very subject with good Chief Max Seiler a few minutes ago, and I told him even the best of us have unspeakable evil lurking inside, and it only takes the right catalyst to bring out such evil. And you, Wilbur Donovan, were my catalyst. You won't be happy to learn I'm now probably more vicious than even as vile creature such as you are. You see, I have a highly developed brain and a very vivid imagination, two important elements you lack in your stupid little primitive thug's mind."

Donovan spat a bloody wad across the short distance landing it square on Bill's cheek. "Oh my! That certainly was uncalled for, Wilbur," Watkins said. "I should have expected as much from an animal like you. You almost ruined a very good moment in my video documentary. That's right, Wilbur; I'm filming everything we're doing here so soon millions can enjoy it after you're gone. Now unfortunately I'm going to have to edit that minor distraction out of the film. You should be ashamed of yourself."

Wilbur readied himself to launch another ball of phlegm, but before he could do so, Watkins backhanded him across the face. Then he reached over onto a stainless steel table covered with what looked like an assortment of tools and surgical instruments and ripped a long strip of duct tape from a roll placing it across Donovan's reddening mouth.

"There. That's much better. Now you'll have to behave. Not to worry, Wilbur, I'll remove it later when it is time for you to scream. And let's not forget about when it's time for you to eat. You see I have a very special meal planned for you. Now don't look at me that way, Wilbur. It's not your last supper, at least not yet, and I wouldn't poison you. I plan to keep you alive for a very long time and suspect you'll beg for death long before you actually do perish. Or should I say mumble for death, since you can't actually talk any longer? Now let me see, first things first."

Watkins reached over to the table and found a wooden dowel about eighteen inches long and about an inch in diameter. The top end of the dowel had been sanded into a smooth round shape. The lower end of the dowel was fitted into a bicycle hand gripper. Watkins examined it closely before securing it into a vice attached to the table. He ran his hand all along the body of the dowel occasionally touching up the surface with a small piece of fine sand paper.

Without another word, he put on a pair of latex surgical gloves and a long white lab coat. He picked up pruning shears from the table turned and walked toward the bound man. Next, in one quick motion, he reached down and grabbed the end of Donovan's penis in his left hand pulled it quickly toward him and with the shears in his other hand neatly snipped the organ off as close to the man's body as possible. Blood poured from the wound, and Donovan moaned in agony behind the duct tape, tears spilling down his cheeks eyes bulging from his reddened face. Watkins immediately picked up a sewing needle and thread sat down on a metal step stool in front of Donovan and started suturing the wound closed without, of course, the benefit of anesthetic.

"There now," Watkins finally said, "I have to make sure you're all sewed up nicely so you don't bleed to death. I've got too many more special things planned for you." Once he saw the bleeding had stopped, Watkins treated the area with generous amount iodine, which once again sent Donovan into fits of muffled screaming, his body thrashing from the burning agony. "Now, Wilbur, it's very important we treat this with the proper medication. We can't have you getting a staph infection."

He turned and winked at the camera saying, "Get it? Staff infection? No? Bad joke? Too soon? Whatever."

Next he proceeded to turn the severed organ slowly inside out rolling it backward while with a surgical scissors he snipped and cut rendering a completely hallow skin of what it once was. Looking over at Donovan, he noticed the man was unconscious.

"Humm." Watkins said into the camera, "It appears Mr. Donovan was unable to endure the pain and has passed out. I suspect he'll be doing a lot of that before we're all finished here. That's probably for the best as I have some side work to do."

Using a remote control unit and watching the monitors Watkins zoomed in on the stainless steel worktable where he proceeded to take the inverted severed penis and carefully unfolded it like a condom, stretching it tightly over the wooden dowel. Once it was expanded as far as it would reach, he took a staple gun and stapled the bottom of the organ securely to the dowel. Behind him, Donovan awoke looking dazed and disoriented. His eyes opened wide with fearful recognition as he once again became aware of his surroundings.

"Just in time! Welcome back, Wilbur. Good to see you back among the living; although you probably won't enjoy living very much, when you experience my next bit of entertainment. I racked my brain for weeks on this one trying to figure out what would be the right punishment for a rapist and murderer such as you. Lo and behold, I came up with a great two-part exercise. You just experienced the first part; the part I've named 'off with his head,' so to speak. Now you get to enjoy the second part, which I have decided to call the "Deliverance" exercise. You remember the scene from the movie *Deliverance*, don't you? Where the good old boys corner the character played by Ned Beatty. No? Well allow me to refresh your memory." He tore the duct tape from Donovan's mouth. "I want to make sure I can hear this loud and clear. It would be a shame to miss even one second of it."

Donovan's eyes opened wide with terror as he realized what Watkins had planned. Watkins looked at the three monitors then made some final adjustments to the camera via remote control. One screen now displayed a close up of Donovan's face; another was a full body shot of the man and the final monitor showed a close up of Donovan's naked backside.

Watkins walked around behind the man and immediately shoved the flesh-covered un-lubricated dowel deep into Donovan's rectum. The man screamed with misery as repeatedly Watkins thrust the dowel in and out impossibly deeper each time. After only a few initial thrusts, the missing lubricant was no longer a problem as Donovan's blood began to flow freely along the glistening tool of torture. Watkins made sure to get several horrific close-up shots of the assault. All the while the assault was occurring and Donovan was screaming in agony Watkins was laughing like the mad-man he had become shouting "Squeal louder little piggy, squeal louder", doing his own impression of the scene from the movie.

He continued until he was exhausted from the effort; rivulets of sweat running down his forehead his shirt soaked with perspiration under the lab coat, splattered with Donovan's blood. He held up the bloody flesh covered dowel for the camera grinning insanely. Once again, Wilbur Donovan lapsed into unconsciousness, the unbearable pain taking its toll.

Watkins looked into the camera and said, "Looks like our boy Wilbur has once again gone beddie-bye. Not a problem. I have so much work to do; preparing his dinner and doing some serious video editing."

After several hours, Watkins returned to find Donovan once again awake but much more disoriented than before, likely from blood loss. Watkins realized he should have planned to have some of Donovan's blood type available for transfusions, but no one could seriously expect him to think of everything. There was now an incredible stench in the cool room, and Watkins noticed Donovan's bowels and bladder must have let loose during his time of unconsciousness. Dried bloody feces clung to the insides of the man's legs leading downward to a substantial mess on the floor.

Watkins walked over to a garden hose hanging on the wall and began to spray the man with icy water saying, "Luckily I planned ahead and installed a drain in the floor. You see, Wilbur, I've tried to think of everything even though I already realized I missed a thing or two. It's the advantage of being highly motivated and having almost a year to prepare. Maybe if I had more time I might have not missed anything at all. Oh, well, I'm flexible and can adapt."

After the naked man was once again clean and the filth dissolved in the spray flushed down the drain, Watkins took a closer look at the weakened man bound helplessly shivering before him. "No. No. No. This will never do. We need to keep up your strength. I'm not ready for you to die, not just yet. I have much more fun in store for you."

Watkins approached the trembling man with a bowl of a gruel-like substance and a spoon, "Wilbur, I guarantee this will help to restore your strength. It is a special mixture of high-protein components I've devised myself especially for you."

Donovan clamped his lips tightly together preventing the spoon from entering not wanting to sample the peculiar smelling substance.

"Wilbur!" Watkins admonished, "What are you so concerned about! You don't honestly think, I would poison you do you? I told you earlier I wouldn't let you off that easily. Now open up and eat your dinner like a good boy."

Reluctantly the man gave in to his hunger and began gulping spoonful after spoonful as quickly as Watkins could shovel it in. The wounded man grimaced with pain as the food passed over his severed tongue stump. After a few spoonsful, Watkins began to slow the feeding.

"Easy, now, Wilbur; it's been a while since you've eaten anything. You don't want to gulp it down too fast only to end up vomiting it back out again do you? What good would that do?"

After a short while, the bowl was completely empty. Watkins set the bowl down clapped his hands together playfully and announced. "Alright Wilbur, let's take a little break and watch a special video I put together for your entertainment."

With a press of the computer keyboard one of the large monitors displayed what appeared to be a 1960's era television show complete with cheery melodious string filled background music. The title "Cooking With Bill" scrolled onto the monitor with the subtitle, "With your host Bill Watkins."

Watkins appeared on the screen standing behind a stainless steel table in a lab coat and Chef's hat. The table held a number of mixing bowls several different sauces, utensils, condiments and a food processor.

"Good afternoon everyone and welcome to this week's show," the Watkins on the video said cheerfully. "Today we'll be making a high-protein snack especially designed to rejuvenate and give back depleted energy."

Donovan watched feebly barely able to focus as Watkins' cheery droning practically lulled him to back to unconsciousness.

"Pay attention, Wilbur!" Watkins insisted, "The best part's coming up." Donovan's eyes opened wide with revulsion as he watched Watkins on the video screen put Donovan's severed tongue into the food processor then peel his bloody, severed penis from the wooden dowel and drop it in as well. Incredibly, Watkins then poured a cup of Donovan's own blood into the processor.

On the monitor, Watkins said with feigned surprise, "Oh! Oh! The recipe said to add some nuts. Where in the world will I ever find some nuts? Oh yes, there are two nice ones."

Next, the video cut to a scene with Watkins approaching the unconscious Donovan with a serrated kitchen knife. Bending down in front of the man, Watkins roughly hacked off his scrotum. Donovan watched this with his mouth hanging agape as on the video Watkins took the severed sack and added to the food processor then efficiently began puréeing the contents. Once complete he poured the contents into a bowl, the same bowl he used to feed Donovan earlier. Then he looked right into the camera and said, "Umm. Umm. At Bill's kitchen, you can have everything from soup to nuts."

Upon realization of what he had just consumed, Donovan began to vomit uncontrollably. He convulsed violently rattling his chains and bindings. Again, Watkins hosed him down with the frigid water. The bound man moaned and screamed as best as his mute condition would allow, tears flowing freely from his sunken eyes.

Watkins heard a faint ringing noise in the distance and noticed a red light above the entrance door flashing. Someone was at the front door. Watkins left the room quickly shouting over his shoulder, "Don't worry, Wilbur. I'll be right back, and we can pick up where we left off."

Leaving the room Watkins removed his protective lab coat and made sure his pants and shoes were free of any traces of his activities. On the way to the front door, he stopped quickly to wash his hands and face, making sure they were spotless. He opened the front door and saw Chief Max Seiler standing on his porch for the second time that day in the light of the early evening setting sun.

"Chief Seiler. Please come in. To what do I owe this pleasure?"

Seiler entered and replied matter-of-factly while looking around the room curiously, "I just thought I'd stop by and check how you are getting along since my visit this morning."

"Why. I'm fine, Chief," Watkins said. "As I told you earlier, with your man out there to guard me and with Donovan soon to be recaptured, I have little to fear."

"That's why I'm here again, Bill," Seiler said. "There's been a bit of a complication in our investigation."

Watkins questioned, "What sort of complication?"

"We believe he hasn't actually left the area," Seiler said. "We believe he's close by and he may be coming for you. We found the van used to snatch him abandoned in a lot not more than a mile or so from here."

"Oh, my goodness!" Watkins said feigning surprise. Then he asked, "Do you think he's stayed in the area to come after me? Is what you think?"

"Well, we believe that might be a real possibility," Seiler said. "Actually, with your permission, I'd like to post a man inside of your house with you for your own protection of course."

Realizing what this meant to his plans, Watkins responded, "No. I don't think so, Chief. I'm a stickler for my privacy. If you wish to station another man outside that's fine with me, but I prefer to keep my house to myself."

This troubled Seiler. Again, he felt the same strange apprehension about Bill Watkins. He started to believe maybe there was more to the man than he originally thought. He said, "If that's what you want, then I'll not push the issue for now. As I said, hopefully after we're finished going over the van, we'll have more clues to lead us to the accomplice and then eventually to Donovan. I still hope to nab him within a day or so."

Watkins walked toward the front door opened it and thanked the chief, indicating once again it was time for him to go. "It's late, Chief and I'm exhausted. I'm going to turn in for the night." Seiler wasn't accustomed to someone ordering him around, especially someone whom he was trying to keep alive. Seiler left the house bidding Watkins an abrupt cursory goodbye as he walked out into the rapidly darkening evening.

Watkins shut the front door turned off the porch light and went from room to room turning off all of the lights. Then he went upstairs and turned on the bedroom and bathroom lights; pretending to be getting ready for bed. After a few moments, he turned out the lights then walked through the darkened house to his basement torture chamber.

When he opened the door to the room, he saw Donovan was frantically scraping his wrists within their bindings. Puddles of blood covered the floor. The metal straps Watkins had used to secure his wrists had bitten right through the skin and into the man's wrist bones. He didn't know if Donovan was attempting to commit suicide or was trying to escape. Whatever his reasoning, Donovan had done some irreparable damage and had lost a great deal more blood. Watkins knew if he didn't act quickly, Donovan would bleed to death. He created two tourniquets from some rubber tubing, and using metal rods, he twisted them until the blood flow ceased. Then he secured them from unraveling by nailing them to the wooden rack.

"That was very foolish, Wilbur," Watkins said. "I told you I'm not going to let you die until I'm good and ready to let you die." Watkins grabbed a bottle of hydrogen peroxide and doused both of Donovan's wrists as the man howled in misery.

For the third time that day, Bill got the garden hose and once again hosed off the naked man and washed the blood down the drain. Looking at Donovan, Watkins realized he had made a grave miscalculation. He had hoped to torture the man for many days bringing him close to death, and then reviving him only to inflict more pain. However, reality never followed anyone's plan and was never like the movies or even like anyone's imagination. It was apparent to Watkins Donovan would be dead soon. Perhaps within the hour, and there was nothing he could do about it. As a result, he'd have to make the best of what time he had remaining.

He originally hoped to spend days cutting and skinning the man alive all the while pouring a salt water mixture or iodine over the wounds, but alas, this was not to be. Watkins knew he'd now have to skip right to the final part of his plan. Since Donovan had suffocated his children, Watkins had decided early on suffocation was how Donovan eventually must die. Watkins checked to make sure the cameras were still rolling; then he walked around behind the bound man and placed a transparent plastic sheet over Donovan's face. He pulled it tight and watched on the monitors as the weakened man used every bit of his remaining energy to struggle for his last futile breaths. Under the sheeting, the man's eyes bulged with terror at the realization he was suffocating. Within a few minutes, Wilbur Donovan was dead.

Watkins walked around and sat in front of the computer keyboard for a few moments staring at nothing in particular as if lost in thought. He had waited and planned a year for his retribution, and now that it was over, it seemed to Watkins to have lasted for much too short of a time. However, what was done, was done and likewise he had to finish what he had started.

All through the night, Watkins feverishly worked at the computer cutting and pasting various elements of video footage using sophisticated computer video editing software. He included a special introduction, which he had recorded many months ago detailing how Donovan had murdered his family and how he had plotted and planned his revenge. Then he added a final segment about how he felt no remorse for what he had done. He said he no longer respected the laws of man and he felt he was above such laws. He also said he no longer feared the fires of Hell as he had already been to Hell and back. As soon as the video was completed to his satisfaction, he did two things.

First, he burned a copy of the video onto a DVD writing the title on the face of the disk; "Death of a Psychopath; Birth of Retribution." He placed the DVD into a jewel case along with a folded piece of paper and wrote on a blank label stuck to the front, "For Chief Max Seiler."

Next, he took the entire edited DVD and uploaded it to several dozen different Internet websites he had been scouting for the past year. These were the types of web sites, which would publish virtually anything. He was certain at least one of them would post his video. He guessed most of them would believe it to be a fake, something very realistic but obviously staged. In a few days when the truth came out, however, he suspected it would be the most downloaded video on the Internet and not just in the United States but worldwide.

He didn't care about the fame, which would accompany the publishing of the video, nor did he care if his name would be ruined and he might go down in history as one of the most evil men on the planet. But he did want to plant the seed of an idea. He wanted millions to see what he had done so some of them might get the notion to do something similar.

Then Watkins picked up the DVD and walked out of the room leaving all the lights burning brightly and all the monitors displaying the corpse of Wilbur Donovan hanging limply from the rack his bluish gray face visible under the plastic film. Keeping the lights in the house off he walked up to his bedroom and sat on the bed with the DVD sitting next to him on his left and his 38 caliber revolver sitting on the bed to his right. The sun was rising and morning light began streaming through his bedroom window.

Officer Jeff Barker sat in the patrol car on the street outside of Bill Watkins' home trying desperately to stay awake for just another few minutes knowing Chief Seiler would be stopping by shortly with his replacement. Barker had been sitting outside Watkins house all night and nothing suspicious had occurred, which made it difficult for him to stay awake. After a few moments, he saw the second patrol car turned the corner heading up the street toward him and he breathed a sigh of relief.

"Thank goodness," he said aloud. "Now I can go home and get some sleep." Suddenly the quiet early morning erupted with the sound of a loud gunshot. Within a few seconds, Barker was out of his patrol car heading for the front porch of the house followed close behind by Chief Seiler and Officer Donald Tremont.

The three approached the front door expecting to have to kick it in and were surprised to find it standing a few inches ajar. Seiler gave an unpleasant look at Barker who shrugged his shoulders and whispered, "I tell you, Chief, no one went in there."

They entered the house with guns drawn and quickly cleared the first floor. Seiler signaled for Barker to check out the basement while he and Tremont went upstairs. After just a few moments, Seiler heard Tremont gasp and call his name. Upon entering the master bedroom, Chief Seiler saw Bill Watkins sitting up in his bed a revolver in his dead right hand and his blood and brains splattered all over the wall behind him. As he approached the body, he noticed a jewel CD case next to Watkins with the note scribbled on it in marker saying, "For Chief Seiler."

He opened it and a small hand written note fell from the case. He carefully unfolded it and held it with two fingers on the corners reading it aloud. It said, "I'm sorry for the deception, Chief Seiler, but I had to do this. I told you I wasn't the same man and would never be again. I hope you can learn to understand. Be sure to check in the basement."

No sooner had the words left Seiler's mouth than he heard shouting from downstairs as Jeff Barker came running up the stairs taking them two at a time. The man was frantic. "Chief, Chief. You have to come down to the basement. You won't believe it. I can't . . . I don't understand." Then the man turned and vomited uncontrollably in the corner of the room.

Seiler looked for a moment at his sickened officer then looked down in his hand at the DVD reflecting from its case. The title "Death of a Psychopath; Birth of Retribution" was scrolled on the shining disk. He felt his stomach lurch at the realization of what he would likely find in the basement.

In the months following the discovery of Wilbur Donovan, Watkins had sadly gotten his final wish. Once the news of the torture and murder of Wilbur Donovan hit the wires all of the websites where Watkins had uploaded the video were offering the footage 'round the clock for both viewing and for downloading. The demand was so great some of the lesser-capable websites crashed from the increased traffic beyond their capacity to handle.

Then within a few weeks, the copycats began to emerge. All over the world, police found corpses of known criminals bound and tortured in abandoned buildings. More and more videotapes started showing up online. New dot com websites began to spring up dedicated specifically to such videos, with titles such as "Watkins' Way," "Retribution," "Getting Even" and "Bill Watkins" dot com.

One of the sites coined a new term, "BW" to reflect the name and actions of the late Bill Watkins. The term quickly spread among the subcultures replacing the term "Going Postal" as a favorite expression used to indicate someone going crazy and wreaking havoc. It soon became the most commonly used metaphor to indicate getting even. People who felt they needed to get retribution would often say they were going to "Go BW" on someone else. Even Hollywood got in on the action with many less-credible studios producing their own series of retribution-style films glorifying such actions.

If there was anything positive to say about the worldwide phenomenon, it was that it resulted in the elimination of many evil people from the planet. However, the negatives outweighed the positives. There were many botched attempts where the criminals had overpowered their captures killing them and escaping. There were many cases of mistaken identity where innocent people wrongly accused ended up suffering intolerable torture and eventual death at the hands of their alleged victims.

Hardcore Bill Watkins devotees chose to follow his method to the letter of the law and commit suicide, afterward leaving heart-broken and grieving relatives. For a while the world, itself seemed to go a little bit crazy then as with all things this too passed.

Chief Seiler sat in his office in the Ashton Police department staring at the DVD lying on his desk. He, of course, had watched it the day they found Watkins' body six months ago, but he chosen never to watch it again. It had remained in his desk drawer all this time. Now that the fervor had died down and everyone had pretty much forgotten about Bill Watkins, it was time to add it to the evidence box and tuck it away forever.

Seiler took the DVD and placed it in the box before sealing it and writing the day's date on the tag. He looked out at the traffic moving briskly along Centre Street and said aloud, "I hope you got what you wanted, Bill. And I hope you've found your peace although I suspect not."

ABOUT THE AUTHOR

Thomas M. Malafarina (www.ThomasMMalafarina.com) is an author of horror fiction from Berks County, Pennsylvania. To date he has published six horror novels *Ninety-Nine Souls, Burn Phone, Eye Contact, Fallen Stones, Dead Kill Book 1: The Ridge of Death* and *Dead Kill Book 2: The Ridge Of Change*, as well as four collections of horror short stories: *Thirteen Nasty Endings, Ghost Shadows, Undead Living* and most recently *Malaformed Realities Volume 1*. He has also published a book of often strange single panel cartoons called *Yes I Smelled It Too; Cartoons For The Slightly Off Center*. He will be releasing *Malaformed Realities Volume 2* and *Volume 3* in 2017, along with rewrites of *Ninety Souls* called *What Waits Beneath, Burn Phone* retitled as *Burner* and *Thirteen Nasty Endings* renamed *Thirteen Deadly Endings*. All of his books are published through Sunbury Press (www.Sunburypress.com).

In addition, many of the more than one hundred short stories Thomas has written, have appeared in dozens of short story anthologies and e-magazines. Some have also been produced and presented for internet podcasts as well. Thomas is best known for the twists and surprises in his stories and his descriptive often gory passages have given him the reputation of being one who paints with words. Thomas is also an artist, musician, singer and songwriter.

CPSIA information can be obtained
at www.ICGtesting.com
Printed in the USA
BVHW032201160220
572538BV00001B/3

9 781620 067949